WINNING BACK
HIS WIFE

WINNING BACK HIS WIFE

BY
MELISSA McCLONE

MILLS
BOON

First published in Great Britain 2013
by Mills & Boon, an imprint of Harlequin (UK) Limited.
Large Print edition 2013
Harlequin (UK) Limited, Eton House,
18-24 Paradise Road, Richmond, Surrey TW9 1SR

© Melissa Martinez McClone 2013

ISBN: 978 0 263 23680 4

Harlequin (UK) policy is to use papers that are natural, renewable and recyclable products and made from wood grown in sustainable forests. The logging and manufacturing process conform to the legal environmental regulations of the country of origin.

Printed and bound in Great Britain
by CPI Antony Rowe, Chippenham, Wiltshire

For Elizabeth Brooks

Special thanks to: Dave Tucker,
John Scurlock, Terri Reed and Jennifer Shirk.

CHAPTER ONE

DR. CULLEN GRAY trudged through the Wy'East Day Lodge, his sore feet entombed in climbing boots he couldn't wait to remove. His muscles ached after two grueling days on Mount Hood. But whatever he'd been through was worth it.

A climber had been rescued.

That trumped a night spent in a warm, comfy bed, a hot shower in the morning and a homemade breakfast complete with scrambled eggs, chicken-apple sausage and buttermilk pancakes with huckleberry syrup.

The smell of coffee wafted in the air, the aroma tickling Cullen's cold nose and teasing his hungry, grumbling stomach. A jolt of caffeine would keep him going long enough to survive the rescue debriefing and the short drive home to Hood Hamlet.

Twenty feet in front of him, members of Oregon Mountain Search and Rescue, OMSAR, sat at a long cafeteria table with coffee cups in front of them. Backpacks, helmets and jackets were scattered on the floor.

Almost there.

Cullen was looking forward to taking off his backpack and sitting, if only for the length of the debriefing.

He passed a group of teenagers, students at the Hood Hamlet Snowboarding Academy, who laughed while they took a break from riding. A little girl, around six years old and dressed in pink from her helmet to her ski boots, wobbled away from the hot-chocolate machine holding a cup with both hands.

A few hours ago, a life had hung in the balance, cocooned inside a rescue litter attached by cables to a hovering helicopter. But down here, lower on the mountain, everything had continued as usual, as if what run to take on the slopes was the most important decision of the day. He much preferred being up there, though not because of any element of danger or adrenaline rush. He took only calculated risks to help others and save lives.

Cullen lived simply in the quaint, Alpine-inspired village of Hood Hamlet. Work and the mountain comprised his life. Sometimes it was enough, other times not even close. But days like today reminded him why he did what he did, both as a doctor and as a volunteer mountain rescuer. Satisfaction flowed through his veins.

A successful mission.

It didn't get much better than that. Well, unless the climber hadn't fallen into the Bergschrund crevasse to begin with. But given the distance of the fall, the climber's serious injuries and the technical nature of the rescue, Cullen thought Christmas magic—something Hood Hamlet was famous for—had been in play even though it was May, not December.

Either that or plain old dumb luck.

Cullen preferred thinking Christmas magic had been involved. Luck seemed too…random. He might be a doctor, but living here for almost a year had opened his mind. Not everything could be explained and proven scientifically. Sometimes patients defied their diagnosis and survived with no logical explanation.

As soon as he reached the table, he shrugged off his backpack. Gear rattled inside. Carabiners clinked on the outside. When the straps left his shoulders, relief shot straight to his toes.

The pack thudded against the floor. The sound echoed through the cafeteria and drew a few glances from the skiers, riders and tourists.

Let them look. Complain even. Nothing, not even his tight muscles or tiredness, could ruin this day.

He removed his black parka with the white block letters spelling RESCUE on the sleeve, tucked it under one of the outside straps of his pack, then sat.

His feet felt as if they were sighing in delight at not having to support any weight.

"Nice work up there, Doc." Bill Paulson, another volunteer with OMSAR, sat on the opposite side of the table. He passed Cullen a cup of coffee from the extras sitting between them. "What you did in the Bergschrund to save that guy's life…"

Cullen bent over to loosen his boots. He didn't like anyone fussing over what he did, let alone another mountain rescuer. He didn't want the praise. The result—a life saved—was payback enough. "All in a day's work."

"Maybe in the emergency department, but not down inside a crevasse." Paulson raised his cup. "I'm buying the first round at the brewpub tonight."

A beer was in order after this mission. "You're on."

Zoe Hughes, the pretty wife of OMSAR team leader Sean Hughes and an associate member herself, stood behind Cullen. "Want anything?"

Heat from the coffee cup warmed his cold fingers. "This is all I need right now."

"Let me know when you want a refill." Her wide smile reached all the way to her blue eyes. "Rumor has it you were a real hero up there today."

He shifted in his seat. Some considered mountain rescue a reckless pursuit, but nothing could be further from the truth. Rescuer safety was the priority, no matter what the mission. "Just doing my job."

She touched his shoulder. "Sean doesn't think he's a hero, either. But you're all heroes. What you guys do, who you are, is the very definition of the word."

"Damn straight. That's why we always get the girls." Paulson winked. "You're going to be my wingman tonight, Gray. We're going to get so many numbers we'll need more memory for our cell phones."

Paulson, a firefighter with Hood Hamlet Fire and Rescue, had a reputation of being a player. No one would accuse Cullen of being one. He had never expected to be living like a monk, but he had a good reason. One that would end soon enough. Until then…

He stared into his coffee, black and strong, fighting memories and resentment.

Going out and doing anything other than drinking a beer and eating a burger didn't appeal to Cullen in the slightest. The one woman he wanted didn't want him. Time to move on. He understood that. He'd come to terms with it. But he saw no reason to frustrate or tempt himself with something he couldn't have right now. He lifted his cup. "You'll get those phone numbers whether I'm there or not."

"True that," Paulson agreed. "But think of the fun we'll have together. Just so you know, I'm partial to blondes. Though I don't mind brunettes or red-heads."

Zoe shook her head, her long hair swaying back and forth. "One of these days you're going to have to grow up and realize women weren't put on this planet solely for your enjoyment."

Paulson flashed her a charming grin. "Not going to happen."

Zoe grimaced. "Too bad, because love does conquer all."

"Love sucks," Paulson countered before Cullen could echo the sentiment.

"Sometimes." A sigh seemed poised to float away from her lips at any moment. "But other times it's pure magic."

Yeah, right. Cullen sipped his coffee. Love caused nothing but heartache and pain. He'd stick with Christmas magic.

Zoe went to refill someone else's cup. The din of conversation increased, and so did the number of people in the cafeteria. More rescue-team members arrived. A photographer snapped pictures. Someone placed a plate of cookies on the table. It had to be getting closer to briefing time.

He checked his watch. "What's taking so long?"

Paulson grabbed a chocolate chip cookie from

the plate. "Hughes must still be outside talking to reporters."

Cullen wasn't a big fan of the media when it came to the way they covered and dramatized rescue missions on Mount Hood. Whenever anything went down on the mountain, reporters and news trucks raced to the rescue operation's base at Timberline Lodge, eager to capitalize on some poor soul's misfortune to increase ratings, web-page hits or circulation.

His stomach growled. He reached for an oatmeal raisin cookie. "Better Hughes than me. I want no part of that feeding frenzy."

Paulson snickered. "Once the press finds out who was lowered into the Bergschrund..."

"How about we say it was you?" Cullen bit into his cookie.

"I'm game," Paulson said. "Especially if the hot blond reporter from Channel Nine wants to talk to me again."

Cullen took another bite. Tasted like one of Carly Porter's cookies. Her husband had been on the mission, too. Jake owned the local brewing company and brewpub. A pint of Porter's Wy'East Lager, with Paulson buying, would hit the spot tonight.

Sheriff's Deputy Will Townsend approached the

table with Sean Hughes at his side. Concern clouded their gazes. Worry was etched in their features.

Cullen wrapped his hands around his coffee cup. He hoped the climber hadn't taken a turn for the worse on the helicopter ride or at the hospital. The guy was married with two young kids.

"Hey, Doc." Will tipped his deputy's hat. "Cell phone turned off?"

"Battery died." Cullen wondered what his cell phone had to do with anything. He placed his cup on the table. "Not a lot of places to recharge up there."

Will's eyes darkened. "We've been trying to reach you."

The deputy's words tightened Cullen's throat. He recognized the serious tone and steady cadence. He'd used both when delivering bad news at the hospital. "What's going on?"

"You're listed as Sarah Purcell's emergency contact."

Hearing the name startled Cullen. His coffee spilled, spreading across the table. "Damn."

Paulson grabbed napkins. "No worries, Doc. I've got it."

Cullen stood and faced the deputy. "What about Sarah?"

The deputy's prominent Adam's apple bobbed up and down. "There was an accident on Mount Baker."

"Accident?" Cullen asked.

A muscle twitched at Will's jaw. "The details are sketchy, but it appears Sarah was at the crater rim when a steam blast occurred. She was hit by rock and fell a significant distance."

Shock reverberated through Cullen's body. His vision blurred. The world tilted sideways.

A hand tightened around his arm. "Steady, Doc." Hughes.

"Deep breaths," another voice said.

Paulson.

Cullen felt himself being seated.

Sarah. Please, God, not her.

His emotions swirled like a whirlpool. Fear and dread spiraled, one on top of the other. Nightmares from another time joined in. Images of his twin brother, Blaine, flashed with strobe-light intensity until Cullen thought his head would explode. He forced himself to breathe. "Is she…?"

What was happening? He was a doctor. Death was something he saw almost every time he worked a shift at the hospital. But he couldn't bring himself to say the word.

Will leaned forward. "Sarah's at a hospital in Seattle."

Not dead. A hundred pounds of anxiety melted away from each of Cullen's bone-weary shoulders.

Tears of relief pricked his eyes. He hadn't seen Sarah in months. Cullen had wanted her out of his life, but he hadn't wanted anything bad to happen to her.

Will named one of the top trauma centers in the Pacific Northwest.

Cullen blinked, gaining control in an instant. He'd done his residency there. Sarah would receive top-notch treatment, but he needed to make sure it was the right care. A good thing Seattle was only a four-hour drive away.

He stood, nearly toppling over before he could catch his balance. Tired. He was tired from the mission. "I've got to go."

Hughes steadied him. "Not so fast."

"We've been getting updates," Will explained. "Sarah is in surgery again."

Again. Not good. Cullen's hands fisted. Surgery could mean anything from pinning a fracture to relieving pressure on the brain. Volcanoes weren't safe places. Being a volcanologist had put Sarah in danger, but no serious injuries had resulted. Bumps, bruises, a few stitches. But this…

Cullen dragged his hand through his hair. He was a doctor. He could handle this. "Any prognosis yet?"

Hughes touched Cullen's shoulder with the strength of a rescue leader and the compassion of a friend. "She's in critical condition."

A snowball-size lump burned in his throat. While he'd been on the mountain saving a life, Sarah had been fighting for hers. Bitter-tasting regret coated his mouth. Oh-so-familiar guilt, too. He hadn't been able to help Blaine. Cullen had to help Sarah.

He couldn't waste any more time. Sarah needed someone with her, and he was all she had.

Cullen grabbed his pack. "I've got to get to Seattle."

Hughes touched his shoulder again. "Johnny Gearhart has a plane. Porter's making arrangements. I'm going to drive you home in your truck so you can change and pack a bag, then we'll get you there. ASAP. I promise."

A protest sat on the tip of Cullen's tongue. He hadn't lived in Hood Hamlet long, unlike several of these guys who'd grown up on the mountain. He'd climbed and drunk beer and watched sports on television with them, but he relied on himself and didn't ask for help. He didn't need help. But Sarah did. He swallowed the words he normally would have said and tried a new one instead. "Thanks."

"That's what friends are for," Hughes said. "Let's go."

Cullen nodded once.

"I'm in." Paulson, carrying his gear, fell into step with them. "So Sarah… Is she family? Your sister?"

"No," Cullen said. "Sarah's my wife."

* * *

Where am I?

Sarah Purcell wanted to open her eyes, but her eyelids felt as if they'd been glued shut. No matter how hard she tried, she couldn't open them.

What was going on?

Something pounded. It took her a minute—maybe longer—to realize the pounding was coming from her head. Maybe she shouldn't try opening her eyes again.

Her head wasn't the only thing hurting. Even her toenails throbbed. But the pain was a dull ache as if it were far off in the distance. Much better than being up close and personal like a battering ram of pain pummeling her.

She'd been hurting more. A whole lot more. This was…better.

White. She'd been surrounded by white.

Cold. She'd been so cold, but now she was warm. And dry. Hadn't she been wet? And the air… It smelled different.

Strange, but it felt as if something were sticking out of her nose.

Beep. Beep. Beep.

She didn't recognize the noise, the frequency of the tone or the rhythm. But the consistent beat made her think of counting sheep. No reason to try opening her eyes again. Not when she could drift off to sleep.

"Sarah."

The man's voice sliced through the thick fog clouding her brain. His voice sounded familiar, but she couldn't quite place him. Not surprising, given she had no idea where she was or why it was so dark or what the beeping might be.

So many questions.

She parted her lips to speak, to ask what was going on, but no words came out. Only a strangled, unnatural sound escaped her sandpaper-dry throat.

Water. She needed water.

"It's okay, Sarah," he said in a reassuring tone. "You're going to be okay."

Glad he thought so. Whoever he might be.

She wasn't sure of anything. Something told her she should care more than she did, but her brain seemed to be taking a sabbatical.

What had happened?

Clouds had been moving in. A horrible noise had filled the air. Swooshing. Exploding. Cracking. The memory of the teeth-grinding sound, worse than two cars colliding on the freeway, sent a shudder through her.

A large hand covered hers. The warmth of the calloused, rough skin felt as familiar to Sarah as the voice had sounded. Was it the same person? She had no idea, but the touch comforted and soothed. Maybe now she could go back to sleep.

"Her pulse increased." Concern filled his voice. He seemed to be talking to someone else. "Her lips parted. She's waking up."

Not her. He couldn't mean her.

Sarah wanted to sleep, not wake up.

Someone touched her forehead. Not the same person still holding her hand. This one had smooth, cold skin. Clammy skin.

"I don't see a change," another man said, a voice she didn't recognize. "You've been here a long time. Take a break. Eat a decent meal. Sleep in a real bed. We'll call if her condition changes."

The warm hand remained on hers. Squeezed. "I'm not leaving my wife."

Wife.

The word seeped through her foggy mind until an image formed and sharpened. His eyes, as blue as the sky over Glacier Peak on a clear day, had made her feel like the only woman in the world. His smile, rare to appear but generous when it did, had warmed her heart and made her want to believe happy endings might be possible, even if she'd known deep in her heart of hearts they didn't exist. His handsome face, with its high forehead, sculpted cheekbones, straight nose and dimpled chin, had haunted her dreams for the past year.

Memories rushed forward, colliding and overlapping with each other, until one came into focus.

Cullen.

He was here.

Warmth flowed through her like butter melting on a fresh-from-the-oven biscuit.

He'd come for her. Finally.

Urgency gripped Sarah. She wanted—no, needed—to see him to make sure she wasn't dreaming.

But the heavy curtain, aka her eyelids, didn't want to open. She struggled to move her fingers beneath his hand. It had to be Cullen's hand, right? Nothing happened.

A different machine beeped at a lower frequency. Another machine buzzed.

Cullen.

Sarah tried to speak again, but couldn't. Whatever was stuck in her nose seemed to be down her throat, too. No matter. She was so thankful he was with her. She needed to tell him that. She wanted him to know how much…

Wait a minute.

Common sense sliced through the cotton clogging her brain.

Cullen shouldn't be here. He'd agreed divorce was

the best option. He no longer lived in the same town, the same state as she did.

So why was he here?

Sarah forced her lips apart to ask, but no sound emerged. Her frustration grew.

"See," Cullen said. "Something's going on."

"I stand corrected, Dr. Gray," the other person said. "This is a very good sign."

"Sarah."

The anxiety in Cullen's voice surprised her as much as the concern. She tried to reconcile what she was hearing. Tried and failed. She wanted to believe he cared about her and that even if they'd both given up on marriage, their time together hadn't been so bad he'd wanted to forget about everything.

Maybe if she could open her eyes a little she could let him know that.

Sarah used every bit of strength she could muster.

A slit of light appeared. So bright. Too bright. She squeezed her eyes shut.

The light disappeared as darkness reclaimed her, but the pounding in her head increased. No longer far away, the pain was in her face, as if someone were playing Whac-A-Mole on her forehead.

She gritted her teeth, unsure if the awful growling sound she'd heard came from her. Everything felt surreal, as if she were a part of some avant-garde indie film. She wanted out. Now.

"It's okay, Sarah. I'm right here." Cullen's rich, warm voice covered her like one of his grandmother's hand-sewn quilts. "I'm not leaving you."

Not true. He had left her.

As soon as she'd mentioned divorce, he'd moved out of their apartment in Seattle, taking everything of his except the bed. After completing his residency, he'd taken off to Hood Hamlet, Oregon. She'd finished her PhD at the University of Washington, then accepted a postdoctorate position with MBVI—Mount Baker Volcano Institute—in Bellingham, a town in northwest Washington.

Another memory crystalized.

Sarah had been developing a program to deploy additional seismometers on Mount Baker. She'd been trying to determine if magma was moving upward. She'd needed more data. Proof one way or the other. Getting the information meant climbing the volcano and digging out seismometers to retrieve data. Putting in expensive probes that provided telemetered data didn't make sense with their limited funding and the volatile conditions near the crater.

The crater.

She'd been at the crater rim to download data to a laptop and rebury the seismometer. She'd done that. At least, she thought so. Everything was sort of fuzzy.

Apprehension rose. Anxiety escalated.

The rotten-egg scent of sulfur had been thick and heavy in the air. Had she retrieved the data or not? Why couldn't she remember?

Machines beeped, the noise coming faster with each passing second.

She tried to recall what had happened to her, but her mind was blank. Pain intensified, as if someone had turned up the volume to full blast on a television set, then hidden the remote control.

"Sarah." His voice, sharp-edged like fractured obsidian, cut through the hurting. "Try to relax."

If only she could. Questions rammed into her brain. The jackhammering in her head increased tenfold.

"You're in pain," Cullen said.

She nodded.

The slight movement sent a jagged pain ripping through her.

Her throat burned. Her eyes stung. The air in her lungs disappeared when she exhaled. Inhaling, she could hardly take a breath. A giant boulder seemed to be pressing down on her chest.

"Dr. Marshall."

Cullen's harsh tone added to her discomfort, to her fear. Air, she needed air.

"On it, Dr. Gray."

Something buzzed. Footsteps sounded. Running. Wheels clattered against the floor. More voices. She couldn't hear what they were saying, nor did she care.

She gasped for a breath, sucking in a minuscule amount of air. The oxygen helped. Too bad the hurting more than doubled.

Make it stop. Please, Cullen. Make it...

The fear dissipated. The pain dulled. The boulder was lifted off her. By Cullen? He used to take such good care of her, whether she wanted him to or not. If only he could have loved her....

Floating. Sarah felt as if she were a helium-filled balloon let loose and allowed to float away in the sky. Up, up toward the fluffy white clouds. But she didn't want to go yet. Not until... "Cull..."

"I'm right here, Sarah." His warm breath fanned her cheek. "I'm not going anywhere. I promise."

Promise.

The word echoed through her fuzzy brain.

Promise.

They'd promised to love, honor and cherish each other until death do them part. But Cullen had withdrawn from her, putting his heart into his all-consuming work and nothing into her. He'd seemed so stable and supportive, but he wasn't as open as she'd originally thought, and he'd held back emotionally. Still, they'd shared some wonderful times and adventures together. A year living in Seattle. Climbing, laughing, loving.

But none of that had mattered in the end. She'd brought up divorce, expecting at least to discuss their marriage. Instead, he'd said okay to a divorce, confirming her fear that he regretted his hasty decision to marry her. Not only had he been willing to let her go without a fight, but he'd been the first one to leave.

That was why she couldn't believe Cullen was promising to stay now. Maybe not today, but tomorrow or the next day or the day after he would be gone, leaving her with only memories and a gold wedding band.

The knowledge hurt, a deep, heart-wrenching pain, worse than any physical pain she'd endured.

I'm not going anywhere.

A part of her wished Cullen would remain at her side. A part of her wished marriage vows were more than words exchanged in front of an Elvis impersonator. A part of her wished love…lasted.

But Sarah knew better. She knew the truth.

Nothing ever lasted. No one ever stayed. Even when they promised they would.

CHAPTER TWO

CULLEN LOST TRACK of time sitting in Sarah's hospital room. His friends returned to Hood Hamlet after driving his truck to Seattle so he'd have transportation. They supported him via text and phone calls. His family offered to come, but he told them no. They didn't need more grief in their lives, and that was all they would find here, in spite of Sarah's progress.

This small room, four walls with an attached bathroom, had become his world except for trips to the cafeteria and a few hours spent each night at a hotel. And his world revolved around the woman asleep in the hospital bed.

He rubbed his chin. Stubble raked his fingertips.

Maybe that was why this felt so strange. He was married to Sarah, but she'd stopped being his wife nearly a year ago. In Hood Hamlet she hadn't existed. At least not to anyone he knew. Not until her accident.

He rose from his chair, wishing he could be anywhere but here. Not even the familiar artificial lighting and antiseptic smells brought him comfort. He'd spent more time at hospitals than anywhere else the past six years—longer if he counted his four years at medical school. But nothing could quiet the unease tying his stomach in figure-eight knots.

His anxiety made no sense.

Sarah's condition wasn't as serious as her initial prognosis had indicated. Antibiotics had cured an unexpected infection and fever. The nasogastric tube had been removed from her nose. Her cuts had scabbed over. The incisions from her surgeries were healing. Even her closed-head injury had been relatively minor, with no swelling or bleeding.

Surely that had to mean…something. Time to settle matters between them? Cullen wanted to close this chapter in his life.

The woman lying in the hospital bed looked nothing like the beautiful, vibrant climber he'd met at the Red Rock Rendezvous—an annual rock-climbing festival near Las Vegas—and married two days later. He wanted this injured Sarah to replace the image he carried in his heart—make that his head. Her long chestnut-colored hair, clear green eyes, dazzling smile and infectious laughter had been imprinted on his brain along with memories of hot kisses and passionate nights. She was like one of those adrenaline-rushing, stomach-in-your-throat, let-me-off-now carnival rides. The kind of ride that looked exciting and fun from a distance, but once on, made you wonder what you'd been thinking when you handed over your ticket.

That had been his problem with Sarah. He hadn't been thinking. She'd overwhelmed him. Too bad he couldn't blame eloping on being drunk. Oh, he'd been intoxicated at the time—by her, not alcohol.

Cullen crossed the room to the side of her bed.

He'd been trying to forget Sarah. He wanted to forget her. But thoughts of her entered his mind at the strangest of times—on the mountain, at the hospital, in bed. But he knew what would stop that from happening—divorce.

After the divorce things will be better.

These past months the words had become his mantra when he was frustrated or lonely.

Sarah's left hand slipped off the edge of the bed. That didn't look comfortable. He placed her arm back on the mattress. Her skin felt cold.

Cullen didn't want her to catch a chill. He pulled up the blanket and tucked it under her chin.

Sarah didn't stir. So peaceful and quiet. Words he would never have used in the past to describe her. She'd been fiery and passionate, driven and always up for a challenge or adventure. Nothing, not even the flu, had slowed her down much.

The silence in the room prodded him into action. Staring at Sarah wasn't what the doctor ordered. Her doctor, that was. Dr. Marshall hadn't wanted her to sleep the day away—not that Sarah could with nurses coming in and out. But she hadn't been too coherent when she woke up, and then she'd drifted back to sleep like a newborn kitten.

Might as well get on with it, Cullen thought. If she followed the same pattern, she wouldn't be awake for long. "Rise and shine, Lavagirl."

Saying her nickname jolted him. He used to tease her about being a volcanologist until he realized she loved the piles of molten rocks more than she loved him.

He would try again. "Wake up."

Sarah didn't move. Not surprising, given her medications. If he kept talking she would wake up.

"So I…" Cullen had tried hard not to miss her. After what she'd done to him, he shouldn't miss her. He'd missed the sex, though. A lot. But he was only human—emphasis on the *man* part of the word. "I've been thinking about you."

He'd told families that talking to patients was important. Now the advice sounded stupid. But when it came to Sarah, he'd never been very smart.

Keep talking, Doc.

He struggled for something to say. His resentment

toward her ran deep. Maybe if he started at the beginning of their relationship when things had been better this wouldn't feel so awkward. "Remember that first night in Las Vegas, you wanted our picture taken in front of the slot machines? We got the photo, but we also got thrown out of the casino."

The two of them had stood on the sidewalk laughing, unsure of the time because of the neon lights. Her laughter had rejuvenated his soul. She was so full of light and love he couldn't get enough of her.

"You looked up at me. Mischief gleamed in your pretty green eyes."

He'd been enchanted, transported back to the time when freedom and fun reigned supreme, when he and Blaine had been impulsive and reckless, goading each other into daredevil challenges and stunts, believing they were untouchable.

"Then you kissed me."

Changing all the plans he'd had for his life in an instant. He hadn't been able to think straight from that moment on. He hadn't cared. Being with her was a total rush. An adventure. Perfect. Nothing else mattered.

"The next night we strolled past the Happily Ever After Wedding Chapel on the strip. You joked about going inside and making things official."

She'd said if they eloped now he couldn't forget

about her when they returned to Seattle or leave her standing at the altar after she wasted years of dating him and planning their big wedding. He'd promised he would never leave her like that.

The affection in her eyes had wiped out whatever brain cells remained in his head. For the first time since Blaine's descent into drugs, Cullen had felt whole, as if the missing piece of him that had died with his twin brother had been found in Sarah.

"I couldn't let you get away."

Cullen had pulled her through the chapel's double glass doors. Forgetting about his vow to take only calculated risks in the future, he'd dived in headfirst without doing his due diligence and performing a cost-benefit analysis. He hadn't weighed the odds or considered the consequences of marrying a woman he knew nothing about.

Common sense couldn't override his heart. She'd made him feel complete in a way he'd never thought he'd feel again. He'd been downright giddy when she'd accepted his impromptu proposal. Thirty minutes and $99 later, they walked out wearing matching plain gold bands and holding a marriage certificate.

A whim? A mistake?

More like a regret.

He'd remembered back in December, when everyone was kissing under the mistletoe in Hood Hamlet and he was alone. That was when it hit him. He'd wished he'd never been introduced to Sarah Purcell.

But Cullen had. He'd married her. That was why he was here now. They were husband and wife until a judge declared otherwise. But he couldn't wait to be free, to get his life in order and put his plan back in place. He was scratching one thing off the list, though. He sure as hell wasn't getting married again. Been there, done that—no need to repeat that particular disaster.

At least he would have Paulson to hang with. The guy was a confirmed bachelor, if there ever was one.

But until Cullen's divorce was final he was stuck with a wife who'd wanted to talk, to fight, to slice open one of his veins and have him bleed out every single thought and feeling he'd ever had.

After the divorce things will be better.

Cullen sat on the edge of Sarah's bed. He wanted to hate her, but seeing her like this, he couldn't. "Your lips are dry."

He picked up a tube from the bed tray, removed the cap and ran the balm over Sarah's chapped lips. She didn't stir. "Better now?"

As he returned the tube to the table, a movement in his peripheral vision caught his attention. The blanket had slipped. She'd moved her left arm again. "Sarah."

She blinked. Once. Twice. Her eyes opened, looking clear and focused. Her mouth formed a perfect O. "You're still here."

Sarah sounded surprised, but relieved. Her reaction offended him. "I told you I wasn't going anywhere."

She grabbed his hand and squeezed. "You did."

Heat emanated from the point of contact, shooting out to the tips of his fingernails and sparking up his arm. He expected her to let go. Instead she stared at him with wide eyes. The corners of her lips curved upward in a hesitant smile.

O-kay. It was a simple touch. Out of gratitude for his being here. No big deal. Except the heat tingled. It felt good. Too good. Cullen pulled his arm away. "Thirsty?"

She nodded. "Water, please."

He pushed a button on the control device that raised the head of her bed, reached for the cup sitting on the bed tray and then brought the glass to her mouth. He positioned the straw against her lower lip. Even after the balm, her lips were dry and peeling. He remembered how they used to be so soft and moist and taste so sweet.

Don't think about that. There weren't going to be any more kisses, no matter how much he'd enjoyed them in the past.

"Sip slowly," he cautioned.

Sarah did. She released the straw. "Where am I? What happened?"

The roughness in her voice scratched his heart. He held on to the glass of water. That would keep at bay the temptation to brush the hair off her face. "You're at a hospital in Seattle. There was a steam blast on Baker. You got hit by falling rock and fell."

Her mouth quirked. "Did the steam blast continue?"

"No," he said. "But Tucker Samson—he introduced himself as your boss and the head of MBVI—said this could be a sign of an impending event."

Her eyebrows slanted. Beneath the bandage on her forehead, lines formed as if she were deep in thought. "I…don't remember much."

Sarah had a mind like a steel trap and never forgot anything. He didn't blame her for sounding worried. "It's okay. You have a concussion, but it's a closed-head injury. No traumatic brain injury."

His words didn't ease her concern. Panic flickered in her eyes. "I wasn't up there by myself."

"Two others were injured, but they've been released from the hospital. You took the brunt of it. Fell quite a distance."

The words were easy to say now, but the image of Sarah when he'd first arrived at the hospital haunted him. His uselessness then reminded him of trying to help Blaine—who had wanted only to blame Cullen for his drug addiction—and of trying to revive his brother later, after he'd overdosed. Being forced to watch from the sidelines as others took care of Sarah was like having his heart ripped from his chest. He'd felt the same after being pushed away from his unconscious brother when the paramedics had arrived at their parents' house. But Sarah didn't need to know any of that.

A corner of her mouth rose into a more certain smile. "Guess that's why I feel like I've gone nine rounds in a boxing match."

"Mixed Martial Arts seems more your style."

"Yeah, now that you mention it, this does feel more like MMA than a few punches, hooks and jabs."

She hadn't lost her sense of humor. That and her intelligence had been two of Sarah's most appealing traits. She'd had a hot body, too. The hospital gown and blanket covered much of her, but she'd lost weight. Her cheekbones appeared more prominent and she looked smaller, almost fragile, a word he would never have associated with her before.

He pushed the straw toward her lips again. "Drink more."

Sarah took another sip. "I've had enough. Thanks."

"Ice chips will soothe your throat. It has to be sore

from the tube." He placed the cup on the bed tray. "Hungry?"

"No." A question formed in her eyes. "Should I be?"

She sounded nothing like the strong, independent woman he'd married. The vulnerability in her gaze and voice tugged at his heart, twisting him inside out. He wanted to hold her until she felt better and her uncertainty disappeared. But touching her, even out of compassion, wasn't a smart idea. "Your appetite will return soon enough."

"Maybe my appetite doesn't want hospital food."

That was more like his Sarah. Not his, he corrected. "Then your appetite is one smart cookie."

She smiled.

He smiled back.

This conversation was going better than he'd imagined. Maybe the bump on her head had shaken some sense into Sarah. Not that it changed anything between them. "I'll sneak in some decent food."

"I should eat even if I don't feel like it. I need to get back to the institute to look at data."

Her words made him bristle. Sarah was a scientist, first and foremost. Studying volcanoes wasn't a job for her, but a passion. The need to be where the action was happening was as natural an instinct as breathing to Sarah. Her work was for the greater good of science and mankind. If only she cared to put as much effort into her personal relationships.

Into him.

"Other scientists can analyze the data," he said. "You need to recover first."

"I'm the institute's specialist. They need me. Those are my seismometers up there."

"Yours?"

Her lips pursed, but not in the kiss-me-now way she had perfected. "A grant paid for them, but the data… Was the equipment damaged?"

"Tucker said the equipment was recovered. The data from the laptop is being analyzed."

"Thank goodness." She glanced around the room until her gaze landed on the door. "How soon until I can get out of here?"

He held up his hands, palms facing her. "Not so fast."

"We may be able to use the data to figure out what's going to happen on Baker. If we predict an eruption successfully, we can use the same process with other volcanoes and save lives."

Her passion cascaded out. Cullen understood why she was so adamant about her work. He felt the same about his. But he had to play devil's advocate, even if he wanted nothing more than to send her on her merry way to Bellingham. "A concussion is only one of your injuries."

Sarah looked down at herself, as if finally realizing she was more than a talking head. Her eyes narrowed at the cast on her arm. "I can slog up Baker with a sling."

As ridiculous as the image of her doing that was, he could see her attempting it. She would hurt herself more, given the pain medication she was on, if she even survived another fall. "How will you self-arrest if you slip? It's hard enough to dig in an ice ax to stop yourself with two usable hands and arms."

She moistened her lips and lifted her chin with a look of defiance. "I won't need to stop myself if I don't slip."

A smile threatened to appear at her bravado. He pressed his lips together. The last thing he wanted to do was encourage her. "You suffered internal injuries, a collapsed lung, broken ribs and an arm fracture. Not to mention you've had two surgeries."

"Surgeries?"

"You have a pin in your right arm, and you no longer have a spleen. Due to the trauma and bleeding, they had to remove it with an open procedure rather than using laparoscopic techniques."

"Oh." Sarah looked as if he'd told her she'd overslept her alarm, not had an internal organ removed through a four-inch incision. "You don't really need a spleen, right?"

A groan of frustration welled up inside him.

Why couldn't she be one of those ivory-tower-type scientists who worked in a lab and never cared if they breathed fresh air or saw sunlight? Then again, he wouldn't have been attracted to someone like that. "You can survive without one."

"That's a relief." She touched her cast. "How soon before I can get back to the institute? Next week?"

Try four to six weeks, if everything went well with her recovery. Most likely six to eight with the surgery. But he reminded himself he wasn't in charge of her medical care. "You'll have to ask your doctor."

Her gaze pinned him. "You're a doctor."

"I'm not *your* doctor."

"You have to have some idea."

Cullen had more than an idea. But he wasn't here as a medical professional. He was here to support her, even if he wasn't part of her life anymore.

He'd been surprised to find out he was her only emergency contact. She'd mentioned her parents to him once, saying they were no longer a part of her life. He supposed the blank line on the employment form had needed a name, any name. No one ever thought the person listed would be contacted. "More than a couple of weeks."

She rubbed her lips together. "Guess I'd better talk to my doctor and find out."

"Once you know—"

"You'll go home," she finished for him.

She wanted him out of her life. He would be happy to accommodate her. "Yes, but not until you're out of the hospital."

Leaving her alone until then wouldn't be right.

"Thank you." Her voice dropped to a mere whisper. "Thanks for being here. This had to have messed up your schedule."

Sarah's unexpected sincerity curled around his heart and squeezed tight, like a hug. He shifted his weight between his feet. "My schedule doesn't matter."

Her gaze met his with an intensity he knew well. She might look bruised and battered, even broken, but intelligence and strength shone in the depths of her eyes. Her eyes were what he'd noticed first about her when they'd met over morning coffee at a campfire. He wanted to look away, but couldn't.

"Your schedule matters," she countered. "It always has before."

"I don't want you to be alone." That much was true. "You're still my wife."

Her face paled. "My fault. I've been so busy at the institute I never followed through on my end with the divorce. I'm sorry. I'll have to get on that."

After bringing up a divorce, she'd been too busy slogging up and down Mount Baker in the name of research to file the marriage-dissolution paperwork. He'd contacted an attorney. He rubbed the back of his neck. "No need."

Her eyes widened. Her lips parted. "What do you mean?"

A part of him wanted to get back at Sarah, to hurt her the way she'd hurt him.

You're a great guy. You'll make some woman a fantastic husband. But our eloping was impulsive. I acted rashly and didn't think about what I was doing. Or what would be best for you. I'm not it. You deserve a wife who can give you the things you want. Things I can't give you.

Correction. Things she didn't want to give him.

Regret rose like bile in his throat. "I knew you were busy, so once I established residency in Oregon I got things started there."

"Oh." Her gaze never wavered from his. "Okay."

It felt anything but okay to him. The knots in his stomach tightened. His throat constricted. He'd had their entire future planned out. A house, pets, kids. And now...

Putting Mount Rainier, Mount St. Helens, Mount Adams and Mount Hood between Sarah and him had never appealed to Cullen more. "I'll go see if your doctor is around so we…you…can find out when you might be discharged."

He strode toward the door without waiting for her reply.

"Is it okay to get out of bed and use the bathroom?" Sarah asked.

Cullen stopped, cursing under his breath. He needed to help Sarah. But the last thing he wanted was to touch her, to hold her. What if he didn't want to let go?

With a calming breath, he glanced over his shoulder. "Yes, but not on your own. I'll grab a nurse and be right back."

Cullen exited the room. He could have hit the button to call the nurse, but he needed some distance, if only for as long as it took him to reach the nurses' station.

He would let the nurse determine the best way to get Sarah on her feet. If he was pressed into service, so be it. But he hoped the nurse was one of the practical types who would handle things herself.

The less he had to do with Sarah until her release, the better.

Sarah washed her hands in the bathroom sink.

A blond nurse named Natalie hovered nearby. The woman wore blue scrubs, and never stopped talking or smiling. "After surgery and pain meds, it takes a while for your system to get back to normal. But you're doing great already!"

Heat rose in Sarah's cheeks. She wasn't used to being congratulated for using the toilet. Maybe when she was a kid, but knowing her parents, she doubted it. At least Natalie had given her *some* privacy. And it sure beat having Cullen help her, even though he was stationed outside the door.

Don't think about him.

She dried her hands, wishing every movement didn't take so much effort or hurt so much. "Um, thanks. I'm not used to going to the bathroom being a community event."

"Don't be embarrassed. This is nothing compared to labor and delivery," Natalie said. "There's no room for modesty there."

Sarah couldn't imagine. Nor did she want to. Given she had no desire to marry again, she doubted she would ever set foot into labor and delivery. Unlike Cullen. If ever a man was meant to be a father...

An ache deep in her belly grabbed hold of her, like a red-tailed hawk's talons around his prey, and wouldn't let go. She struggled to breathe.

Her incision. Maybe her ribs. She leaned against the sink to allow the pain to pass.

Natalie placed a hand on Sarah's shoulder. "Sit on the toilet."

A knock sounded. "Need help?"

Cullen's voice stopped whatever had been hurting. Sarah straightened. "I'm fine."

Natalie adjusted the back of the gown. "Let's get you back before Dr. Gray gets on me for keeping you away too long. Doctor hubbies are the worst, since they're sure they know what's best for their wives."

Maybe some doctors, not Cullen. He'd looked as if he wanted to bolt earlier. She didn't blame him. This was the height of awkwardness for both of them.

Natalie opened the bathroom door. "Here she is, Dr. Gray."

Sarah shuffled out of the bathroom. She felt each step. An ache. A pain. A squeezing sensation. Nausea, too.

Cullen held his arms out slightly, but he wasn't spotting her as closely as before. Dark circles under his eyes and stubble on his face made her wonder how much sleep he'd been getting. Not much, by the looks of it. But he was still the most handsome man she'd ever seen. That bothered her. She shouldn't be thinking about her future ex-husband that way. Maybe it was the pain medication.

"You're walking better." He sounded pleased.

A burst of pride shot through her. "Just needed to find my legs."

"It's awful when they go missing," Natalie joked. "The two of you should take a short walk down the hall and back. Sarah needs exercise."

Excitement spurted through Sarah. She would love to get out of this room.

Cullen's lips narrowed. He didn't look as if he wanted to go anywhere with her.

Disappointment shot straight to the tips of her toes, even though she knew he had every right to feel that way. Why would he want to spend more time with her than he absolutely had to? She'd hurt his pride by bringing up a divorce. As if shutting her out of every part of his life outside the bedroom hadn't hurt her. But she'd had to do something. It was only a matter of time before he left her. She'd saved them from suffering more hurt in the future.

"You should be walking a few times each day," Cullen said.

Of course he had to say that. He was a doctor. But he'd done enough. She wasn't about to force him into escorting her.

Sarah padded toward the window. "I'll parade around the room. This gown isn't made for walking in public unless I want to flash the entire floor."

"I doubt anyone would complain." Cullen's lighthearted tone surprised her. "Especially not Elmer, the eighty-four-year-old patient two doors down."

Natalie laughed. "Elmer would appreciate it. He's such a dirty old man. But I'm sure you wouldn't mind too much yourself, Dr. Gray."

Cullen winked at the nurse. "Well, Sarah *is* my wife."

Sarah stared at him dumbfounded. Legally she was his wife. But he wanted the divorce as much as she did. Why was he joking around as though they were still together?

He strode to the cupboard resembling a built-in armoire with a drawer on the bottom. "And since I'd rather not have any men leering at her, it's a good thing I bought this."

Sarah had no idea what he was talking about. "What?"

Cullen opened one of the cupboard doors and pulled out something orange and fuzzy. "This is for you."

She stared in disbelief at a robe. "I…"

"I hope orange is still your favorite color," he said.

She was touched he remembered. "It is."

Natalie clapped her hands together. "How sweet!"

His gesture sent a burst of warmth rushing through Sarah. This was so…unexpected. She cleared her throat. "Th-thanks."

"Now your backside will be covered, and I won't have to get into any territorial pissing matches." He held up the robe so she could stick her left arm through the sleeve. "Let's drape this over your right shoulder and not bother your cast."

Sarah nodded, not trusting her voice. She appreciated Cullen staying with her at the hospital, but his company was enough. She didn't want him buying her anything, especially something as lovely and as thoughtful as this robe.

He tied the belt around her waist. "Now you're set."

She didn't feel set. She felt light-headed. Chills ran up and down her arms. Neither had anything to do with her injuries, but everything to do with the man standing next to her.

"Ready?" he asked.

No, she wasn't.

"Go on," Natalie encouraged. "You can do this."

No, Sarah didn't think she could.

Cullen extended his arm toward her. She reached for his hand, unsure if touching him would hurt or not.

He laced his fingers with hers, sending tingles shooting up her arm. "It'll be okay."

Chills and tingles were not okay.

"I won't let you fall," he said confidently.

Sarah had no doubt he would catch her if her body gave out and gravity took over. But who would stop her heart from falling for him? Or catch her if it did?

CHAPTER THREE

THE LAST THING Cullen had expected to become was Sarah's walking buddy, but that was what happened over the next three days. His reluctance gave way to anticipation for the after-meal strolls through the hospital corridors. He'd wanted to be here and help her. This offered him the perfect opportunity to do both.

They didn't discuss the past. They barely mentioned the future unless it related to her recovery. Sometimes they didn't say much at all. It was enough to be with her, supporting her. Enough, he realized, for now.

As they walked through the hospital's atrium full of tall trees and flowering plants, Cullen held Sarah's hand. A satisfied smile settled on his lips. "You did have the energy to make it down here."

"Told you so. This is much better than walking the hallways upstairs." Sarah glanced up at the skylights. The ends of her long chestnut hair swung like a pendulum. Her bruises were fading, more yellow and brown than blue. "I can't wait until I can go outside."

"It won't be long." Sarah looked better, healthier. He squeezed her hand. "You're getting stronger every day."

Her green eyes sparkled. "It's all this exercise."

He wished it was because of him.

Yeah, right. He wasn't foolish enough to think this time together meant anything. These walks were about her health, nothing else. "Exercise can be as important as medication in a patient's recovery. So can laughter."

She grinned wryly. "That's why you wanted to watch the comedy show last night."

"You laughed."

"I did. And I'm smiling now."

"You have a very nice smile."

"Thanks." She glanced at their linked hands. "Do you think I could try walking on my own?"

Cullen had gotten so used to being her living, breathing walker, holding her hand had become second nature. But it wasn't something he should get used to, even if it was…nice. He released her hand. "Go ahead."

Sarah took a careful, measured step. And another.

He flexed his fingers, missing the feel of her warm skin against his. "Tomorrow you'll want to hop on a bike instead."

Her lips curved downward in a half frown, half pout. "I like our walks."

"Me, too."

Her smile, as bright as a summer day at Smith Rock, took his breath away. He rubbed his face. Stubble pricked his hand. He'd been in a rush to get to the hospital and forgotten to shave again.

"But I have to be honest." She looked around, as if seeing who might be listening. "I'm ready to escape this joint."

"I don't blame you." Except once she left, everything would go back to the way it had been. They would live separate lives, in separate states. The realization unsettled him. "You should be released soon."

"Has Dr. Marshall mentioned a discharge date?"

The anticipation in her voice made Cullen feel foolish for enjoying this time together. She wanted a divorce. He wanted one, too. "No. But given your progress, Dr. Marshall might have one in mind. Ask him when he makes his rounds."

Hope danced in her eyes. "I will."

Sarah took another step, swaying. She stumbled forward.

"Whoa." Cullen wrapped his right arm around her waist and grabbed her left hand. "Careful."

She clutched his hand. "I lost my balance."

If that was the case, why was she leaning against

him with her fingers digging into his hand? But he liked the way she clung to him. "This is the longest walk we've taken. Let's head back to your room."

He expected an argument. Instead she nodded.

Sarah loosened her grip and flexed her hand. "I can make it on my own."

He laced his fingers with hers. "I know, but humor me anyway."

She held on to his hand. "I suppose that's the least I can do after all you've done for me."

A list of what he'd done for her the past two years scrolled through his mind. "I suppose it is."

Sarah owed him, and he would gladly take this as payback. He wasn't about to let go of her. And that had nothing to do with how good having her close felt. He caught a whiff of her floral-scented shampoo. Or how good she smelled. Nothing at all.

That afternoon, Sarah gripped the edge of the hospital blanket. She stared at Dr. Marshall, wondering if she'd misunderstood him. She sure hoped so. "Don't you mean an independent discharge?"

"An independent discharge is not going to happen." Dr. Marshall looked like a grandfather, rather than one of Seattle's top surgeons, with his silver-wire-frame glasses and thinning gray hair, but the man was turning out to be the devil in disguise. "You are unable to care for yourself. Your discharge planner and orthopedist agree."

She hadn't been waiting all afternoon full of hope only to hear this. "That's…silly."

Cullen, who leaned against the far wall near the window, gave a blink-and-you'd-miss-it shake of his head.

Her fingers tightened on the fabric, nearly poking through the thin material. She didn't like being so aware of Cullen's every movement. Her senses had become heightened where he was concerned. She'd wondered if he felt the same way. Now she knew.

No!

Frustration tensed her muscles, making her abdomen hurt more. Disappointment ping-ponged through her. They'd shared lovely walks though the hospital, holding hands like high-school sweethearts. She'd assumed Cullen would support her independent-discharge request, but he hadn't. He didn't want her returning to her apartment in Bellingham to stay by herself.

"Nothing about this is silly," Dr. Marshall said. "You are lucky to be alive."

"Damn lucky," Cullen murmured.

She didn't feel that way. Nothing but bad luck could have put her at the crater rim when a steam blast occurred, something that hadn't happened on

Mount Baker in nearly four decades. Now she was stuck in the hospital with only her soon-to-be ex-husband for company when she needed to be at the institute figuring out if the event was a precursor to an eruption or just the volcano letting off steam as it had done in 1975. "*Silly* was the wrong word to use, but I'm not an invalid. I'm getting around better."

Dr. Marshall gave her the once-over. "There's a big difference between walking the hallways and being capable of caring for yourself."

"You overdid it this morning," Cullen added, as if dumping a carton of salt onto her wounds helped matters.

"I know I have a way to go in my recovery." She would be doing fine once the pain of her incision and ribs lessened. The throbbing in her head, too. "But I don't need a nursemaid."

A knowing glance passed between Dr. Marshall and Cullen.

Sarah bit the inside of her cheek.

"No one is suggesting a nursemaid. But I agree with Dr. Marshall. You're right-handed." Cullen's gaze dropped to her cast. "Dressing yourself, doing anything with your left hand, is going to take some adjustment. Not to mention your sutures and ribs. You'll need assistance doing most everyday things. There will also be limitations on lifting and driving."

Maybe she shouldn't have expected Cullen to take her side. But even with his lack of support now, she had no regrets. Bringing up a divorce was better than waiting around for him to do it. And he would have. People always walked away. He would walk away from her once she was out of the hospital, leaving her alone. Again.

The sinking feeling in her stomach turned into a black hole, sucking her hope down into it.

No, she couldn't give in and admit defeat. The institute relied upon her expertise. Others had been looking at the data since the steam blast, but volcanic seismology was her specialty. She couldn't let people down. It wasn't as if she had anything else in her life but her work. She glanced at Cullen, then looked away. "I don't care if it hurts. I'll figure out a way. I need to get back to the institute. I have a job to do."

"Is your current health and your long-term health outlook worth risking for your job?" Dr. Marshall asked.

Sarah raised her chin. "If it means determining how to predict a volcanic eruption, then yes. It's worth it."

A muscle ticked at Cullen's jaw. "If you return to the institute too soon, you won't be doing them or yourself any favors."

She saw his point, even if she didn't like it. "I'll be careful."

"What does your job entail, Sarah?" Dr. Marshall asked.

"Analyzing data."

"After she climbs Mount Baker to gather it," Cullen added. "Or am I wrong about that, Dr. Purcell?"

Of course he wasn't wrong. From his smug grin he knew it, too. That was why he'd used her title. "I can send a team up to download the data."

Maybe that would appease him—rather, Dr. Marshall.

"Are you able to work remotely from home?" Dr. Marshall asked.

Sarah would rather be at the institute, but she would take what she could get. "Telecommuting is an option. I have internet access in my apartment."

Dr. Marshall looked her straight in the eyes. "Is there someone who can stay at your apartment and care for you?"

Sarah's heart slammed against her chest so loudly she was sure the entire floor of the hospital could hear the boom-boom-boom. Even though she knew the answer to his question, she mentally ran through the list of coworkers at the institute. Most would be happy to drop off food or pick up her mail, but asking one to stay with her would be too much. She couldn't impose on any of them like that.

She'd never had a close friend, a bestie or BFF she could count on no matter what. Her life had been too transitory, shuttled between her parents and moving frequently, to develop that kind of bond with anyone. Not unless you counted Cullen. She couldn't. It wouldn't be fair to either one of them.

She chewed on her lower lip. "I could hire someone."

"Home care is a possibility," Dr. Marshall said.

Fantastic. Except her studio apartment was tiny. The floor was the only extra place to sleep, the bathroom the only privacy. She hated to admit it, but home care wouldn't work.

"If Sarah's in Bellingham, nothing will keep her from going to the institute or heading up the mountain if she feels it's necessary," Cullen said matter-of-factly.

She opened her mouth to contradict him, but stopped herself. What he said was true.

"You know I'm right," he said.

It annoyed her that he knew her so well.

"Is that true?" Dr. Marshall asked her.

She tried to shrug, but a pain shot through her. "Possibly."

Cullen laughed. The rich sound pierced her heart.

One of Cupid's arrows had turned traitorous. "A one-hundred-percent possibility."

No sense denying it. He'd had her number a long time ago.

Dr. Marshall gave her a patronizing smile, as if she were a five-year-old patient who would appreciate princess stickers rather than a grown adult who wanted him to work out her discharge. "My first choice in cases involving a head injury, however minor, is home care by family members, but Dr. Gray has explained your situation."

Sarah assumed Dr. Marshall meant their marriage, since Cullen was the closest thing to family she had. She wasn't an orphan. Her parents were alive, but they'd chosen their spouses over her years ago. "I'm on my own."

"That leaves a sniff. A skilled nursing facility," Dr. Marshall explained. "We call them SNFs. There are several in the Seattle area."

Cullen's smile crinkled the corners of his eyes, making her heart dance a jig. So not the reaction she wanted to have when she was fighting for her freedom. Independence. Work.

"That sounds like a perfect solution," Cullen said.

Maybe for him. In Bellingham she had access to the institute and her own place to live. Down here in Seattle, she had…nothing. But what choice did she have? Sarah swallowed her disappointment. "I suppose. As long as I have my laptop and access to data."

Dr. Marshall adjusted his wire-framed glasses. "Many SNFs have Wi-Fi."

Might as well look on the bright side. "That's better than dial-up."

"Your concussion will make it difficult for you to concentrate for any length of time." Cullen sounded so doctorlike. Totally different from the man who had helped her back to her room this morning. "If you push too hard, you may experience vision problems and headaches."

"I'll use a timer to limit my computer usage," she offered.

"No symptom is a one-hundred-percent certainty, but Dr. Gray is correct. You don't want to do too much too soon," Dr. Marshall said.

Something about his tone and eye movement raised the hair on her arms. "What exactly am I going to be allowed to do?"

"Rest and recuperate," Dr. Marshall said, as if those two things would appeal to her.

R & R was something a person did when they were old. Not when the second-most-active volcano in the Cascades might erupt. "The SNF sounds like my only option, but you might as well put me out of my misery now, because—"

"You'll die of boredom," Cullen finished for her.

In their one-plus year of marriage—over two if you counted the time they'd been separated—he'd figured her out better than anyone else in her life. That unnerved Sarah.

Dr. Marshall adjusted his glasses. "A few weeks of boredom is a small price to pay."

Small price? The SNF sounded like an institutional cage. She'd be locked away and forced to sleep or "rest." She stared at the cast on her arm.

Lucky to be alive. Maybe if she kept repeating the words she would believe them. Because right now life pretty much sucked.

"There is another option," Cullen said.

Her gaze jerked to his. The room tilted to her left as if she were standing in a mirrored fun house. She closed her eyes. She must have walked too far earlier. When she opened them everything was back where it belonged, and Cullen was staring at her with his intense gaze.

She swallowed the lump of desperation lodged in her throat. Anything would be better than a nursing facility. "What other option?"

"Come home with me to Hood Hamlet."

Her mouth gaped. The air rushed from her lungs.

"I have Wi-Fi," Cullen continued, as if that made all the difference in the world. "I promise you won't be bored."

No, she wouldn't be bored. She would be struggling to survive and keep her heart safe.

Here at the hospital, people came in and out of her room. She and Cullen were never alone for long. He left each night to go to his hotel. What would it be like if it were only the two of them?

Dangerous.

Sarah tried to speak, but her tongue felt ten sizes too big for her mouth, as if she'd been given a shot of Novocain at the dentist's office. But she knew one thing....

Going home with Cullen was a bad idea. So bad she would rather move into the SNF and die of boredom or stay in the hospital and die of starvation or go live in a cave somewhere with nothing but spiders and other creepy-crawly things for company.

Having him here made her feel warm and fuzzy. Taking walks reminded her of how comfortable they'd once been together. But she couldn't rely on him to be her caretaker. She'd been vulnerable before they'd separated. She would be totally at his mercy in his care. If she found herself getting attached to him, or worse, falling in love with him all over again...

He would have the power not only to break her heart, but shatter it. She couldn't allow that to happen.

Cullen wore a digital watch, but he swore he heard the seconds ticking by. He braced himself for Sarah's rejection. He'd offered her a place to recover, but she'd reacted with wide-eyed panic, as if she was about to be sentenced to life in prison.

Stupid. Cullen balled his hands with a mix of frustration and resentment. He should never have made the suggestion. But she'd looked so damn miserable over the idea of the SNF, he'd had to do something. A good attitude was important in a patient's recovery. He didn't want her to experience any setbacks. Skilled nursing facilities had their role in patient recovery, but Sarah was better off elsewhere. He knew that as a trained physician. He knew that in his gut.

But no one was going to step up and offer Sarah an alternative. No one except him.

And she hadn't even cared. At least not according to her anything-but-that reaction.

Might as well get the word *sucker* tattooed on him. He'd let their pleasant walks and hand-holding soften him up.

A buzzing sound disturbed the silence.

Dr. Marshall checked his pager. "I have to go. Tell

the nurse your decision and have her relay it to me and the discharge planner."

The surgeon strode out of the room without a glance back.

The minute the door shut, the tension in the air quadrupled. Cullen had faced challenges working as a doctor and as a mountain rescuer, but he'd never felt more out of his element than standing here with his wife, a wife who didn't want him for a husband. Not that he wanted her, either, he reminded himself.

Sarah toyed with the edge of her blanket. Her hands worked fast and furiously, as if she were making origami out of cloth.

The silence intensified. Her gaze bounced from her cast to the colorful bouquet of wildflowers from MBVI to everything else in the room. Everything except him.

Hard to believe that at one time they were so crazy about one another they couldn't keep their hands or lips off each other. Now she couldn't bear to look at him.

He hated the way that gnawed at him. Time to face the music, even if a requiem played. "I'm only trying to help. Give you another choice."

"I'm surprised you'd want me around."

Her words cut through the tension with the precision of a scalpel. He was about to remind her she had been the one to ask for the divorce, but held his tongue because she was right. He didn't want her around because she messed with his thoughts and his emotions, but he had to do the right thing here, whether he liked it or not. "I want you to recover. Get you feeling better and back on your feet in the shortest amount of time possible. That's all."

She studied him as if she were trying to determine what type of volcanic rock he might be. "That's nice of you."

Her wariness bugged him. "We've been getting along."

Her lips parted. She pressed them together, then opened them again. "It's just..."

He hated the hurt lying over his heart. "Would it be that awful for a few weeks?"

"No, not awful," she admitted. "Not at all."

Her words brought a rush of relief, but added to his confusion. "Then what's the problem?"

"I don't want to be a burden."

A burden was the last label he'd use for her. "You're not."

"You've put your life on hold this past week."

"I won't have to do that when I'm in Hood Hamlet. I can get back to work and my mountain-rescue unit."

Sarah moistened her lips. "I didn't think I was supposed to be alone."

"Friends have offered to help."

Her gaze narrowed. "So you won't be around that much?"

"I work twelve-hour shifts at the hospital. The rescue unit keeps ready teams stationed on the mountain in May and June."

"Oh."

That single word didn't tell him much. He rocked back on his heels. "So what do you think?"

"I appreciate the offer."

"But—?"

Sarah squinted. "I…I don't know."

Her uncertainty sounded genuine. He had expected to hear a flat-out *no*.

She sank into her pillow. "Is it something I need to decide right now?"

"Dr. Marshall wants you to tell the nurse your decision. Arrangements have to be made if you choose a SNF."

She rubbed her thumb against her fingertips.

"Attitude plays a role in healing," he continued. "Hood Hamlet will be better for you in that regard."

"Give me a minute to think about it."

Cullen didn't know why she needed more time or why he was trying so hard to convince her. Yes, he wanted to do the right thing, but her decision changed nothing. If she refused his offer, the next time they saw each other… They wouldn't be seeing each other unless she challenged the divorce terms. The way it would have been if she hadn't had her accident.

The bed dwarfed her body, making her look small and helpless. Strange, given she was the strongest women he knew next to Leanne Thomas, a paramedic and member of OMSAR.

Sarah grimaced.

Two long strides put him at the side of her bed. "Your head."

She gave an almost imperceptible nod. "I may have overdone the walking today."

His concern ratcheted. "Does anything else hurt?"

"Not any more than usual."

Using the back of his hand, he touched her face. She wasn't flushed, but a temperature could mean another infection. "You don't feel warm."

She closed her eyes. "My brain might be rebelling from having to work again. Think I probably need another nap."

"Probably."

But Cullen preferred to err on the side of caution. He checked the circulation of each finger sticking out from her cast. He wanted to blame his anxiousness on the Hippocratic oath, but he knew there was more to it than that. The *more* part revolved around Sarah. He wished it weren't so. In time he hoped—expected—not to care or to be so concerned about her. Time healed all wounds, right?

She opened her eyes. "You always had a nice bedside manner."

He didn't want her words to mean anything. He hated that they did. "It's easier with some patients."

"With me?" she asked, sounding hopeful.

"Yes."

Sarah's lips curved into a slight, almost shy smile. "Thanks."

He brushed hair off her face. "You're welcome."

Her eyelids fluttered like a pair of butterfly wings.

He remembered when she'd slept against him and her eyelashes had brushed his cheek. The urge to scoop her up in his arms and hold her close was strong, but he couldn't give in to temptation. This woman had trounced his heart once. Whatever else he did, he couldn't let himself fall in love with her again.

"I'm not trying to be difficult," she said softly.

"You're being yourself. I wouldn't expect any less."

But he expected more from himself.

Seeing Sarah injured and hurting brought out his

protective instincts, but he had to be careful. He had to be smart about this, about her.

She'd claimed to love him right up to the day she brought up divorce. She'd lied about her feelings and let him down in the worst possible way.

He didn't trust her. He couldn't. No matter what she might do or say.

Memories and feelings he'd thought he'd buried deep kept surfacing. He liked keeping his emotions under wraps, but he found it much too easy to lose control around Sarah. He couldn't wait for her to turn down his offer so he could be done with her.

She stared at him. "I don't need any more time to decide. My goal is to recover as soon as possible. My apartment is too small for a caretaker to stay with me. A SNF would be too impersonal."

The implication of her words set him on edge. "So that means…?"

"I'll go to Hood Hamlet with you. If that's still okay?"

It wasn't okay, not with the way Cullen was feeling right now. His heart pounded and his pulse raced, as if he'd run to the summit of Hood post-holing through four feet of fresh snow. An adrenaline rush from physical activity, no problem. Adventures with calculated risks, fine. The way he was reacting to Sarah? Unacceptable.

Still, Cullen had made the offer. He wouldn't go back on his word. But he would have to keep a tight rein on his emotions and remain in control. He clenched his teeth. "It's fine."

CHAPTER FOUR

GET SARAH HOME. Get her well. Get her back where she belonged.

Driving to Hood Hamlet on Highway 26, Cullen focused on the road and tried to ignore the woman seated next to him. Not an easy thing to do with the scent of her sweet, floral shampoo tickling his nostrils. He grasped the leather-covered steering wheel with his hands in the ten and two o'clock positions, exactly as he'd been taught in driver's ed.

He'd rarely driven this way as a teenager. "Hell on Wheels" best described his brother's and his driving styles back then. But after Blaine had overdosed, Cullen prided himself on doing things, including driving, the right way, the correct way, to make things easier on his grieving parents. He'd made some stupid mistakes in the past, but he hoped he wouldn't make any more where Sarah was involved.

As he pressed harder on the accelerator to pass a semitruck, he fought the urge to sneak a peek at her. He'd done that too many times since leaving Seattle. Concentrating on the road in front of him was better. Safer. He flicked on the blinker to return to his own lane.

"You haven't touched your milk shake," Sarah said.

The meaningless, polite conversation of the past four hours made him wish for a high-tech transporter beam that could carry them to the cabin in less than a nanosecond. He'd settle for silence, even the uncomfortable kind of quiet that made you squirm while you struggled to think of something to say. He stretched his neck to one side, then the other. "I'm not that thirsty."

Cullen hadn't had much of an appetite since last night. He hadn't slept much, either, tossing and turning until the sheets strangled him like a boa constrictor. He rolled his shoulders to loosen the bunched muscles.

"You're missing out. My chocolate milk shake is delicious."

Sarah sounded as though she was smiling. A quick glance her way—he couldn't help himself—showed she wasn't. Her lips were tight.

She stirred her drink with the straw. "Thanks for suggesting we stop."

Making stops along the way had allowed her to walk around and change positions, but had added time to the drive. "You needed to stretch your legs."

Their final stop hadn't been all about Sarah. The

truck had felt cramped. Confined. He'd needed some fresh air and space.

"If you'd rather have chocolate, we can trade." She held out her cup to him. "I like vanilla."

Memories of other road trips to rock climb flashed through his mind. Stopping to buy two different kinds of milk shakes had become the routine. Sharing them during the drive had been the norm. Pulling over to have sex had been his favorite break. Hers, too.

Whoa. Don't go there. He tightened his grip on the steering wheel. "Thanks, but I'm good."

"Suit yourself, but I'm willing to share."

Her lips closed over the end of the straw sticking out of the cup. She sipped. Swallowed.

His groin twinged. Blood boiled. Sweat coated his palms.

Damn. He needed to cool off. Quickly. "I'm happy with mine."

Cullen snagged his milk shake from the cup holder and sucked a mouthful through the straw. The cold vanilla drink hit the spot. A few more sips and his temperature might return to normal.

He was much too aware of her—from the way she glanced sideward at him to the crooked part in her hair. Things he shouldn't notice or care about.

And he didn't. Care, that is.

But now that she was an arm's distance away, her feminine warmth and softness called to him like a PLB, personal locator beacon, beckoning in the night. Only, no one was lost. Nothing was lost except the impulsive, reckless side of who he used to be. The side Sarah brought out in him. The side he had buried alongside his brother.

Sure, Cullen missed the sex. What man wouldn't? But he'd been surviving without it. Without her. Celibacy was the better choice for now. Blaine had lost himself in drugs. Cullen had seen what losing control did to a man, to his brother. He wouldn't lose himself in Sarah.

He returned his drink to the cup holder. Maybe if he didn't say anything to her, she wouldn't talk to him.

"Is Hood Hamlet much farther?" Sarah asked.

So much for that tactic. He gritted his teeth. "Twenty-five minutes if we don't hit any traffic."

"That sounds pretty exact."

He'd been checking the clock on the dashboard every five minutes for the past two hours. "I drive this way to the hospital."

"You work in Portland, right?" she asked.

Great, more small talk. "Gresham. Northeast of the city."

"A long commute."

"Twelve-hour shifts help."

"Still a lot of driving," she said. "Why do you live so far away?"

He tapped his left foot. "I like Hood Hamlet."

"There have to be closer places."

"Yes, but I prefer the mountain."

"Why?"

"It's…"

"What?"

"Charming."

"You've never been one for charming," she said. "You thought Leavenworth was, and I quote, 'a Bavarian-inspired tourist trap on steroids.'"

He had said that of the small town on the eastern side of the Cascade Mountains. "I liked climbing there."

"Nothing else."

He'd liked spending time with her in Leavenworth. A glance at the speedometer made him ease up on the gas pedal. "Hood Hamlet is different."

"Different, how?"

"There's something special about it."

"Special?"

He nodded. "Almost…magical."

She half laughed as if the joke was on him. "When did you start believing in magic?"

He understood her incredulous tone. A year ago he

would have laughed at such a thought himself. After Blaine died, Cullen's belief in any kind of "magic" had died, too. He hadn't believed in anything that wasn't quantifiable—whether it was a diagnosis or a cure. Everything had to have an explanation. The one thing in his life that defied reason—his relationship with Sarah—had blown up in his face. "It's hard not to believe when you're there. A lot of people feel the same way."

"Must be something in the water," she joked.

A trained scientist like Sarah wouldn't understand. He'd been the same way until three things had changed his mind—the rescue of two climbers trapped in a snow cave last November, the town pulling off its Christmas Magic celebration in mid-December and Leanne Thomas getting engaged on Christmas Day. The three events had defied logic, but had happened anyway. "Maybe."

"The mountain air, perhaps," she teased.

"You never know." But he knew it was neither of those things.

"Whatever it is, I hope it's not contagious."

"I have no doubt you're immune as long as Mount Hood remains dormant."

He expected her to contradict him, if only to argue with him. She didn't.

"What else does the town have beside magic?" Sarah asked.

"The people. It's a great community." He'd realized how supportive they truly were with the numerous offers of help following Sarah's accident. "Very welcoming to strangers. That's how I ended up moving there. I'd driven up to Mount Hood on a day off. I had lunch at the local brewpub and met the owner, Jake Porter. When he found out I was involved with mountain rescue in Seattle, he told me about their local unit, OMSAR. He invited me to go climbing, and we did. I met a few more people. One told me about a cabin for rent. Next thing I knew, I was signing my name on a year lease."

"That's serendipity, not magic."

"Semantics," he countered.

"A year lease is a commitment."

"It's worked out fine."

"That's great, but I prefer a month-to-month lease."

Of course she would. A month-to-month marriage would have been her first choice if that had been allowed. "You've always liked to give yourself an out with everything you do."

Sarah stiffened. "I know better than to back myself into a corner."

She'd always been independent, but she sounded defensive, as if the world were against her. He hadn't meant to attack her. "Someone might be there to help you escape."

"I'd rather not deal with the consequences if they're not."

So jaded. He hoped their separation hadn't done this to her. "People can surprise you."

"They usually do, but not in the way I expect."

Cullen wasn't sure what she meant, but the tip of a knife seemed to be pressing against his heart. He wasn't sure he wanted to know the answer, but curiosity compelled him to ask the question. "Does that include me?"

"Yes."

The knife pierced his heart. Her answer shouldn't have surprised him. She was impulsive and impatient with a tendency to erupt like the volcanoes she loved so much. He'd tried to take care of her when they were married, but she'd pushed him away. He'd tried to make her happy, but she never seemed happy enough. A lot like Blaine. Cullen's jaw tightened to the point of aching. "Care to elaborate?"

"You've been great about my accident." Gratitude shone in her eyes. "I wasn't expecting that."

He felt the tension in his jaw ease. "Couples in our situation can be friendly to each other."

She nodded. "Especially when divorce is what we both want."

The knife dug a little deeper into his heart. "It is."

A cheery love song played on the radio. The up-beat tempo was the antithesis of how he felt. He fought the urge to press the power switch so the music would stop.

"I'm glad you found the place you belong," Sarah said.

"Hood Hamlet is the best thing that's happened to me in a long time." He remembered the list he'd put together of places they could live after he finished his residency. Portland had been near the top because of the Cascades Volcano Observatory in nearby Vancouver, Washington, but he'd never considered Mount Hood. And wouldn't have if they'd stayed together. "The only drawback is everyone wants to know everybody's business."

She clucked her tongue. "Typical small town."

"I sometimes forget how small."

"Does that mean people are going to be talking about us?"

He took a deep breath and exhaled slowly. "They already are."

"Why is that?"

Cullen shouldn't have said anything. His stomach roiled.

"Why?" Her voice rose.

His palms sweated. He wiped one on his jeans.

"No one in Hood Hamlet knew I was married until your accident."

Her mouth gaped. She closed it. "Why didn't you tell them?"

He didn't want to admit he'd been nursing a wound so deep when he arrived in town he wasn't sure he would recover. But he had. And he was doing fine until she'd crashed back into his world. "You were no longer a part of my life. I could start over in Hood Hamlet with a clean slate once the divorce was finalized."

The color drained from her face. Hurt clouded her eyes. "You pretended to be single."

Her tone and stiff posture put him on the defensive. "Not intentionally."

She turned toward the window.

"Hey, I'm not the bad guy here." He lowered his voice. "Don't forget you're the one who brought up a divorce."

"True, but you agreed," she countered. "And I didn't move to a new town and act like I was single."

"I didn't act that way, either," he explained.

She stared at her cast with a downtrodden gaze. "Sure you didn't."

"I didn't." Her reaction surprised him. They'd been separated and hadn't seen each other for almost a year. Divorce was a mere formality. "What were people supposed to think? I moved to Hood Hamlet alone. I wasn't wearing a wedding band. No one asked if I'd been married, so I saw no a reason to tell them."

Sarah had grasped her milk shake so hard she'd put a dent in the cup. "If they had asked?"

Not carrying around the baggage of a failed marriage had helped him move on. He'd never expected anyone, including Sarah, to find out. But by trying to make things easier on himself over this past year, he'd made them harder now. For Sarah, too. "I would have told the truth."

She bit her lower lip. "No wonder people are talking."

"Friends were with me when you were in ICU. They had questions."

She lifted her chin. "What do your friends know about our situation?"

"Not much."

"Cullen…"

She sounded more annoyed than hurt. But he wouldn't call that progress. "They know we've been separated for almost a year but are together now."

She drew back with alarm. "Together?"

"For now."

Her mouth twisted.

"While you recover," he clarified.

"Well, I hope it won't take me long to get better so you can make your fresh start in Hood Hamlet and I can get back to Mount Baker."

At least they agreed on something. "Me, too. Except you can't rush through your recovery. If you focus on one day at a time, you'll get to where you're supposed to be."

And so would he.

Then they could both get on with their lives separately.

Cullen couldn't wait for that to happen.

Sarah couldn't wait to arrive in Hood Hamlet. The drive had been uncomfortable and painful to her injuries, but also to her heart. She couldn't change what had happened with Cullen. She could only learn from her mistakes and move forward with her life. That was what she needed to do. He already seemed to have done that. She hated that knowing he'd moved on twisted up her insides.

She stared out the truck's window. The highway snaked up Mount Hood, giving panoramic views of the tree-covered mountainside. The dark green of the pines contrasted with the cornflower-blue sky. Breathtaking. She couldn't get Cullen's image out of her head.

He'd shaved, removing the sexy stubble from his

face. But he still looked totally hot, with the strong profile she knew by heart, warm blue eyes fringed by thick dark lashes that danced with laughter and lush lips perfect for kisses.

Had been perfect. Past tense.

A ballad played on the radio. The lyrics spoke of heartbreak and loneliness, two things she was familiar with.

But Sarah knew she and Cullen were better off apart. He'd found the place he belonged—Hood Hamlet. She'd never had that, not even when they'd lived together. Once she finished her postdoc she would keep looking until she found the haven she'd been searching for her whole life.

After a childhood of being shuttled between parents and stepparents as if she were a smelly dog no one wanted, she didn't need much. Nothing big and fancy, just a place where she belonged and mattered. Where she was loved.

She'd thought she found that with Cullen, but she'd been wrong. After a few months of marriage she'd seen the familiar signs. But she was older and wiser and knew what was going to happen. Only, this time she didn't have to wait to be shuffled off and abandoned. She could be the one to leave before that happened.

Cullen touched her forearm. "Sarah…"

She jumped. The seat belt kept her in place, but her cast hit the door with a thud.

"You okay?" he asked.

Anxiety rose like the pressure building inside Yellowstone's Old Faithful. But Sarah couldn't afford to erupt. She swallowed around the caldera-size lump in her throat. The stronger she appeared, the more in control, the sooner she could return to Bellingham and work. She nodded, afraid her voice might quiver like her insides.

"We're coming into Hood Hamlet," he said.

He flicked on the left-hand blinker. The traffic heading west slowed. He turned onto a wide street. A gas station and convenience store sat on one corner, and trees lined the left side of the road, the treetops glistening in the sun. A short distance away she saw the peaks of roofs.

She didn't believe in magic, but anticipation built over seeing this town Cullen called home.

The truck rounded a curve. Hood Hamlet came into view. Surprise washed over her. It was lovely. Picture-book perfect. Sarah could almost imagine herself in the Swiss Alps, not the Cascades, due to the architecture of the buildings.

"Welcome to Hood Hamlet." Cullen's voice held a note of reverence she understood now. No wonder he wanted to live here.

An Alpine-looking inn resembled a life-size four-story gingerbread house. A vacancy sign out front swayed from a wood post. Flowers bloomed in planters hung beneath each of the wood-framed windows and from baskets fastened on wood rafters. "It's so quaint."

They approached a busier part of the street. He slowed down. "This is Main Street."

A row of shops and restaurants had a covered wooden sidewalk. People popped in and out of stores. A woman with three children waved at Cullen.

He returned the gesture with a smile. "That's Hannah Willingham with her kids, Kendall, Austin and Tyler. Her husband, Garrett, is a CPA and OMSAR's treasurer."

A feeling of warmth settled at the center of Sarah's chest. "*Charming* is the perfect way to describe Hood Hamlet."

"You should see the place at Christmastime. The town goes all out."

Hood Hamlet was made for Christmas, with its mountain setting, ample snow and pine trees. She would love to see it in person. Too bad she would be long gone by then. "It must be wonderful."

"A winter wonderland." His eyes brightened. "There's an annual tree-lighting ceremony after Thanksgiving. The entire town turns out no matter the weather. Wreaths and garland are hung across Main Street. Every streetlight is strung with red and white lights to look like candy canes."

It sounded so inviting and special. Her Christmases had never been like that. No holiday had been. "Is Easter a big deal in Hood Hamlet, too?"

"The town holds an annual egg hunt. It's pretty low-key. Nothing like the shindig my mom and sisters put on. They could teach the Easter Bunny a thing or two," he joked.

She'd found nothing humorous about it. Her hands balled. "Easter at your parents' house was like stepping into the middle of a magazine spread or home-decorating show."

"Holidays are big deals to my family."

No kidding. "Your mom and sisters put Martha Stewart to shame. It was exhausting watching them do so much." Easter with Cullen and his family had shown Sarah how different their childhoods and lives had been. Her parents didn't do much for the holidays. Meals, special occasion or not, were eaten in front of the television or in the car, or they were skipped. She'd planned a wedding that had never happened, but she didn't know how to cook for a huge crowd or be a proper hostess. No way could she be the kind of wife Cullen and his family expected. "I tried to help, but I only slowed them down."

"Yeah, they go all out," he agreed. "I love it."

Cullen's words confirmed what Sarah had realized back then. She would never be able to pass muster with the Grays. Her shoulders sagged. The pain shooting down her right arm matched the hurt in her heart. She forced herself to sit straight.

"Holidays are more down-to-earth in Hood Hamlet, but nice, too. Lots of town traditions," he continued. "Santa and the Easter Bunny have been known to show up on Main Street to have their picture taken with kids and pets."

Pets? He'd never talked about animals before. "Do you have a pet?"

"No, but if I wasn't gone for so long when I work, I might consider getting one."

"I thought you didn't like dogs and cats."

"I like them, but my mom's allergic," he said. "One of the guys on the rescue unit has a Siberian husky named Denali. She's a cool dog."

"Get a cat. They're independent. A good pet for someone who is away a lot. Especially if you have two. That's what my boss Tucker says."

"I don't know if I'm a cat person. I'd like to know a pet cares if I'm around or not."

She knew the feeling. "Cats care, but they don't show it."

"Then what's the use of having one?"

Sarah could have asked him the same question about having a husband. His serious nature and stability had appealed to her when they'd first met. He'd been the exact opposite of the other men in her life, the same men who had disappointed and hurt her. But after they'd married she realized the traits that initially appealed to her kept him from being spontaneous or showing a lot of emotion, leaving her feeling isolated and alone, like when she'd been a kid.

The one emotion he'd had no difficulty expressing was desire. No issues in that department. A heated flush rushed through her, along with more memories she'd rather forget. "You're better off without a pet."

Cullen made a left-hand turn onto a narrow street that wound its way through trees. Homes and cabins were interspersed among the pines.

"This is convenient to Main Street," she said.

"Especially to the brewpub."

Cullen's former mountain-rescue unit in Seattle went out for beers after missions, but call outs hadn't been weekly occurrences. She couldn't imagine rescues were that frequent on Mount Hood. He must like to go out with his friends.

No doubt women were involved. Her left hand balled into a fist. She flexed her fingers. "That must come in handy on Friday and Saturday nights."

"Very handy."

The thought of Cullen with another woman sent a shudder through Sarah. "Who do you go to the brewpub with?"

"Mostly OMSAR members and a few firefighters."

"Nice guys?"

"Yes, but not all are men."

Her shoulders tensed. This was none of her business. Some people dated before a divorce was finalized. She shouldn't care or be upset over what Cullen did.

A quarter mile down the road, he turned the truck onto a short driveway and parked in front of a small, single-story cabin. "This is it."

Sarah stared in disbelief. She'd been expecting an A-frame, not something that belonged in a storybook. The log cabin was delightful, with wood beams and small-paned windows. A planter containing colorful flowers sat next to the front door. "It's adorable. I half expect to see Snow White walk out the front door, followed by the seven dwarfs."

He stopped the truck and set the parking brake. "It was used as a vacation rental so has curb appeal, but I wouldn't go that far."

"You have to admit it's cute."

He pulled the keys out of the ignition. "It suits my purpose."

She opened the passenger door. "I can't wait to see the inside."

"Stay there." Cullen exited, crossed in front of the truck and stood next to her. He extended his arm. "I'll help you inside."

She'd noticed his manners the first time they met. She'd appreciated the gentlemanly behavior. It wasn't something she was used to and it made her feel special. Too bad she hadn't felt as special after they married. Ignoring her soreness, she reached for his hand. "Thanks."

"Go slowly." He wrapped his hand around her waist. "I'll get the luggage once you're settled."

She wasn't about to argue. Not when the warmth of his skin sent heat rushing through her veins. All she had to do was make it to the front door and inside the cabin. Then she could let go and catch her breath.

Cullen escorted her toward the cabin as if she was as delicate as a snowflake. She took cautious steps, fighting the urge to hurry so she could let go of him. The scent of him embraced her. Every point of contact was sweet torture. Relief nearly knocked her over when she reached the porch step.

He squeezed her hand. "Careful."

Yes, she needed to be careful around Cullen. Reactions to him could bring disaster down on her already hurting head.

Reaching around her with his other hand, he unlocked the door. A feeling of déjà vu washed over her. When they'd arrived in Seattle after eloping, Cullen had taken her to his apartment. He'd swept her up into his arms and carried her over the threshold. The romantic gesture had sent her heart singing and told her she hadn't made a mistake eloping.

"It's a good thing Snow White and her crew aren't here, or this place would be too crowded." He pushed open the door with his foot. "Go on in."

No romance today. Sarah hated the twinge of disappointment arcing through her. She released his hand and stepped through the doorway.

The decor was comfortable and inviting. The kitchen was small but functional, with stainless-steel appliances and a tiled island with a breakfast bar. The bar stools matched the pine table and six chairs in the dining room that separated the kitchen from the living room. "Nice place."

A river-rock fireplace with a wood mantel on the far wall drew her attention. She imagined a crackling fire would be nice when the temperature dropped. A large television was tucked into the space above the fireplace. A three-cushion, overstuffed leather couch was positioned in front of the fireplace/TV to the left. The perfect place to relax after a long day. Log-pole coffee- and end tables, as well as photographs and artwork, added a touch of the outdoors to the rustic yet welcoming decor. "You got new furniture."

He closed the door behind him. "I rented this place furnished."

"Did you put your stuff in storage?"

"I sold it."

She glanced around. Nothing looked familiar. "Everything?"

"Most of it was castoffs from friends and family anyway. No sense dragging all that old stuff here with me."

Sarah ignored a flash of hurt. She'd given him a framed photograph from Red Rocks on their first wedding anniversary. And then she remembered. "A fresh start."

"Yes."

"Nice cabin." Much nicer than any place she'd ever lived, including the apartment they'd shared. "I can see why you signed a year lease."

"I'm comfortable here."

If she'd ever wondered if Cullen needed her, Sarah had her answer today. He didn't need her. He had a nice place to live, friends and a good job. His life was complete without her.

Too bad she couldn't say the same thing about her life without him.

CHAPTER FIVE

"SOMETHING SMELLS GOOD."

The sound of Sarah's voice sent a thunderbolt of awareness through Cullen, jolting him back to reality. For the past two hours he'd relished the solitude of the cabin, pretending she wasn't asleep in the guest bedroom. He placed the hot pad on the counter, then turned away from the stove. "Dinner."

She stood where the hallway ended and the living room began with bare feet, tangled hair, looking sleep-rumpled sexy. A half smile formed on her lips. "I didn't expect to wake up to dinner cooking."

He glimpsed ivory skin where the hem of her T-shirt rode up over her waistband. The top button on her jeans was undone, making him think of her shimmying out of them.

Appealing idea, yes. Appropriate, no.

Cullen focused on her face. Still a bit roughed-up after the accident, but pretty nonetheless. "You took a long nap."

"The bed makes the mattress back at the hospital

seem like a slab of granite. I felt like I was sleeping on a cloud."

She'd tended toward the devilish in the past, making it difficult to imagine her as an angel now. "I told you this place would be better than a SNF."

"Yes, you did."

Having her around wasn't turning out to be the best thing for him, though. His gaze strayed to the enticing band of bare skin. The hint of flesh tantalized, reminding him of what had been kept from him. And would never be his again.

He jammed a spoon into the pot of refried beans and stirred.

"I'm glad I listened," she said.

He realized she was wearing the same clothes as earlier. "You can't be comfortable in those jeans. Put on pajamas or sweats."

Shrugging her left shoulder, she studied a photograph of Illumination Rock hanging on the wall.

His stomach dropped. "You can't undress yourself."

Damn. The thought of helping her had never crossed his mind. He'd been thinking about his needs, not hers.

"I probably could if I tried. Natalie told me to leave the button on my jeans undone," Sarah said. "But I didn't think about changing when we arrived. I hit the mattress and was out."

Cullen felt like a jerk. He should have checked on her more carefully. But he hadn't wanted to get too close after the drive.

Good work, Dr. Gray.

The sound of Blaine's voice mocking Cullen, blaming him with a growing list of transgressions, was almost too much for him to take. He lowered the temperature on the beans, then checked the Spanish rice.

He should have done more for Sarah. But he'd needed a break. He might be a physician, but he was still a man. One who hadn't kissed or touched a woman in almost a year. In spite of their marriage falling apart and the hard feelings that brought with it, undressing Sarah would have meant his needing a cold shower.

Cullen would have to get past that. He was responsible for her well-being. "I'll help you after..."

Sarah's face paled.

His stomach roiled. *What the—*

She swayed unsteadily.

Adrenaline surged. Cullen ran.

She slumped against the wall.

He wrapped his arms around her before she crumpled to the ground like a house of cards. "I've got you."

Her warmth, softness and smell were like sweet ambrosia. His groin tightened. He recalled parts of the anatomy…in Latin.

"Thanks." Her breath caressed his neck, sending pleasurable sensations through him. "I was dizzy. I must have gotten out of bed too fast."

He would gladly take her back to bed. And join her.

Bad idea. "You've had a long day. It's been a while since you ate."

"The milk shake—"

"Food."

She straightened. "I feel better now."

"Good, but let's not take any chances." He swept her up into his arms, ignoring her sharp inhalation and how good it felt to hold her. "I don't want you to fall."

As if concern explained the acceleration of his pulse or his breathlessness.

Wariness clouded her eyes. "I don't want you to strain your back."

"Thanks for the concern, but you hardly weigh anything." Sarah had always been fit, but never this thin. He carried her to the couch. "We'll have to put some meat on you."

Sarah's gaze narrowed. "That's not what a woman wants to hear."

As he walked, her breasts jiggled.

Desire slammed into him, hard and fast like a line drive to third base. A fire ignited low in his gut.

Forget the Latin. Organic chemistry equations might work better. "Men like women with curves. Gives them something to hold on to."

Awareness flickered in her eyes. Sarah parted her lips.

All he had to do was lower his mouth to hers and…

"Some men," she said.

If he'd had a thermometer under his tongue, the mercury would have shot out the end and made a real mess. "This man."

Tension sizzled in the air. The physical chemistry between them remained strong, and, if the past sixty seconds were anything to go by, highly combustible.

Fighting the urge to get the hell away from her before his control slipped any further, he placed her gently on the couch. "Rest while I finish getting dinner ready."

He strode to the kitchen with one purpose in mind—put distance between him and Sarah, even if it was less than twelve feet. Attraction or not, this had disaster written all over it. She was injured. She was his soon-to-be ex-wife. Thinking of her as any-thing other than a patient would be…wrong.

Cullen checked the beans and the rice. He glanced at the clock on the microwave. "Time for your meds."

"I'd rather not take them." The back of the couch hid all but the top of her head. "They make me loopy."

"Staying ahead of the pain is important."

"I'm ahead of it."

Not for long. Her voice sounded strained. He filled a glass with water and dispensed her pills. "This isn't up for negotiation."

She poked her head up. "Whatever you're cook-ing smells so good."

"Enchiladas."

"One of my favorites."

Changing the subject wasn't like Sarah. She must not feel well. He carried the water and medicine to her. "Here you go."

She stared at the pills as if they were poison. "Your patients must call you Dr. Hardnose."

He handed her the pills. "They might, but not to my face. Well, except you."

"I'm not your patient." She shot him a chilly look, popped the pills into her mouth and drank the water. "Satisfied?"

"Very. It's not often you do what you're told."

"I only took the pills because you made dinner."

"Then it's a good thing I didn't tell you someone else made the meal."

"Who?"

"Carly Porter." He placed Sarah's water glass on the coffee table. "She stopped by while you were sleeping."

A thoughtful expression crossed Sarah's face. "That sure is nice of Carly."

Sarah's voice sounded tight, almost on edge. A good thing she'd taken her pills. "Carly and her husband are good people. Jake's the one who owns the brewpub."

A corner of Sarah's mouth curved upward in a lopsided smile. "Oh, you mentioned him earlier."

The timer on the oven dinged.

"Dinner's ready," Cullen said. "You can eat on the couch."

"I've been eating in bed. I'd rather sit at the table, if that's okay?"

His stomach twisted. This would be their first meal together since she'd brought up divorce.

She touched her cast. "If you'd rather I eat here—"

"The table works." He was being stupid. Just because the last time had ended badly didn't mean this time would. Hell, he'd wanted to kiss her a few minutes ago. No matter how he looked at this situation, an epic fail seemed imminent. "Give me a sec."

Cullen set the table. Utensils clattered against the plates. His hands shook. He wasn't sure what had gotten into him, but he felt clumsy, a way he wasn't used to feeling.

He placed the hot casserole dish, bowls of rice and refried beans and a bottle of sparkling apple cider on the table. He left the six-pack of Wy'East Brewing Company's Hogsback Ale, courtesy of Jake, in the refrigerator. Cullen needed his wits about him with Sarah here. "Dinner's ready."

He helped her up from the couch, conscious of her every movement and aware of each brush of his skin sparking against hers.

She squeezed his hand. "Thanks."

A lump formed in his throat. He grumbled, "You're welcome," then escorted her to the table. He kept his arm around her in case she became light-headed— yeah, that was the reason, all right—pulled out a chair and helped her sit. His hand lingered on her back.

"Everything looks delicious," she said.

Her lips sure did. What was he doing? Sarah had an excuse for acting loopy. Cullen didn't. He looked away and dropped his hand to his side.

"I can't believe someone made you dinner." She sounded amazed.

He sat across from her, then dished up chicken enchiladas smothered in a green tomatillo sauce. "Carly and Jake did this for you, too."

"No one's ever done something like this for me."

He dropped a spoonful of refried beans onto her plate and then his. "People are helpful in Hood Hamlet."

She motioned to the serving spoon in his hand. "You included."

Cullen added a scoop of the rice. "You'll serve yourself soon enough."

Sarah's shoulders drooped as if someone had let the air out of her. "I'd make a big mess right now, and you'd have to clean up after me."

That was what she'd done with the divorce. Left him to deal with it. He took a sip of the sparkling cider. The sweetness did nothing to alter the bitter taste in his mouth. Maybe a beer wasn't such a bad idea. Just one. He never had any more than that.

"You're smart for serving tonight," she continued.

A smart man would never have allowed his heart to overrule logic so that he ended up marrying a total stranger in Las Vegas. "Just trying to be helpful."

"I...appreciate it."

As they ate, Cullen wondered if she did. She hadn't appreciated what he'd done when they were together.

Bubbles rose in his glass, making him think of champagne. Marriage was like champagne bubbles, first rising in pairs, then groups of three, then individually. He was thankful he and Sarah had skipped the middle part by not having a baby right away. A divorce was bad enough without having to deal with a custody battle. "It's a practical decision. I don't have time for extra chores tonight. I have to work the graveyard shift at the hospital tomorrow night and need to get back into my routine."

Maybe sleeping in his bed at home would give him a restful night of sleep. He hoped so.

She studied him over the rim of her glass. "Who will be my nursemaid?"

"I found the perfect babysitter."

Sarah stuck her tongue out at him.

That was more like it. He grinned. "We could go with *nanny* if you prefer."

She waved her cast in the air. "I bet this thing could do some damage."

"To yourself most definitely."

"Very funny." She feigned annoyance, but laughter danced in her eyes. "So who's stuck here with me first?"

"Leanne Thomas," Cullen said. "I know her from OMSAR. She's also a paramedic."

"Sounds capable."

"I'd trust her with my life. In fact, I have," he admitted. "You'll be in good hands.

"I'm in good hands now."

He appreciated the words, but he'd fallen down on the job this afternoon. "I'm trying to do my best."

"You are," she agreed. "I'm not sure how I'll ever repay you."

"You don't have to." That was the truth. He didn't want anything from her. Well, except to finalize their divorce. Soon… "I remember what it was like."

Wrinkles formed on her forehead. "Remember what what was like?"

"To have a broken arm."

She leaned over the table. "When did you break your arm?"

"I was eleven." He took another enchilada from the pan. "Want more?"

"No, thanks." Sarah stared at him. "I had no idea about your arm. How did you break it?"

"A soccer tournament. This big kid shoved me out of bounds after I scored a goal. I landed wrong and fractured my arm in two places."

"Ouch."

"That's all I could say in between grimacing and crying."

She drew back, as if horror. "You cry?"

"Past tense. I was eleven."

"I'm teasing," she said. "Nothing wrong with crying, no matter what your age."

"Only if you're an emotional, overwrought sissy man."

"Wouldn't want someone to take away your man card."

"Damn straight."

She sipped her cider. "Tell me more about your broken arm."

He patted his mouth with a napkin. "Not much more to tell. It happened in early July, so I spent the rest of my summer in a cast. It sucked."

"You do know how I feel."

He nodded. "I couldn't swim or go in the sprinklers. I wasn't allowed to ride my bike or skateboard. No going on rides at the county fair, either. Casts weren't allowed."

"That must have been the worst summer of your life."

Nope. That was a toss-up between last summer when he was trying to get over her and the summer after his brother died. But her rejection had hurt lots more than his arm fracture. He was relieved he'd moved past that. "It wasn't fun, but I survived. So will you."

His tone came out harsh, without an ounce of sympathy or compassion. He needed to try harder. Apologize. Being with Sarah brought out strong feelings and emotions, ones he would rather forget existed. He'd seen what losing control had done to Blaine. Cullen wouldn't allow the same thing to happen to him.

Forks scraped against plates. Glasses were raised and returned to the table. The lack of conversation was awkward. But Cullen didn't know what to do about it. He'd never known what to do with Sarah except kiss her and take her to bed.

Not an option. Even if a part of him wished it were.

As Cullen loaded the dishwasher, Sarah sat at the table with a plate of cookies within arm's reach. Medication dulled the pain, but made her feel as if she'd drunk one beer too many. Maybe that was why dinner with Cullen had seemed so weird. Forget walking on eggshells—the floor was covered in shattered glass and she kept stepping on the shards.

An uncomfortable silence had enveloped them during the meal. The same unsettling quiet had consumed their marriage. If Sarah could have made it to the guest bedroom on her own, she would have bolted after she'd finished eating. But, since she couldn't, death by chocolate chips sounded like the best alternative.

She bit into a cookie. The sweet flavor exploded in her mouth. "Great cookie."

Cullen glanced over his shoulder. "Carly is known for her baking skills."

"I can see why." Sarah had been surprised about Cullen's broken arm. She wondered what else she didn't know about him. Sex had been the way they'd been able to communicate best. But even that hadn't been enough after a while. Uh-oh. Thinking about sex and Cullen wasn't going to help matters. "I think I'll have another cookie."

"Save me one."

She held her left hand above the plate. "There are over a dozen."

Cullen glanced over his shoulder. Amusement—at least that was what she hoped it was—flashed in his eyes. "I know how much you love cookies."

"You gave me a cookie bouquet for my birthday." That had been five months into their marriage. He'd also covered their bed with rose petals. A romantic gesture when romance had been nonexistent. "They were tasty."

"I never got one."

"That's because you left for your shift at the hospital and I didn't hear from you for two days."

Cullen gave her one of those you-have-to-be-kidding looks. "I had to work."

By the time he'd returned, the cookies had been eaten and the rose petals had wilted. "You never called or texted. Not even during breaks."

He tugged at his collar. "I need to concentrate when I'm at the hospital."

He had never owned up to his behavior in the past. Why had she expected anything different now? Best to forget everything that had happened between them. Good or bad. She pushed the plate of cookies away. "Help yourself. You'll have to roll me back to my room if I eat any more."

"Roll you, carry you." He bent to put something in the dishwasher. "Not much difference."

Maybe not for him.

A wave of helplessness washed over her, threatening to drown her. She hated not being able to do anything on her own. She hated being at someone else's mercy. She hated relying on anybody. Oh-so-familiar disappointment pressed down on her. She had finally been getting everything on track when life threw a rock at her. She didn't want to have to depend on Cullen. She didn't want to end up needing him.

The tight ball of emotion in her belly unraveled like yarn, sending pent-up feelings rolling through her.

She couldn't unsnap her bra or button her jeans or be the kind of wife a man would love forever.

Tears stung her eyes.

Oh, no. Sarah didn't want him to see her like this. She was independent and strong, not needy and emotional. Except, the only thing she felt like doing right now was crying.

She blinked. She looked up. Drops still fell. She dabbed her eyes with the napkin.

Time to get out of here.

Without Cullen's help.

Using her left hand, she pushed against the table. Mantling had always been a favorite climbing move, but this took more effort than she was used to exerting. Her muscles protested. Her abdomen ached. Still she managed to stand, scooting the chair back in the process.

Cullen looked at her. Forks clattered into the sink. He rushed to her side. "What are you doing?"

"I don't need to be rolled or carried." Her voice cracked. "I can do it myself."

Except she couldn't. All she wanted to do was sit. Pride kept her standing.

"I was kidding." He didn't sound amused. His dark eyes looked annoyed. "Like old times."

She raised her chin, but that didn't make up the difference in height. The top of her head came to his nose. She reminded herself that in every other way they were equals. And an underground city of elves lived inside Mount Shasta, too. "The old times weren't that great."

He flinched. "They weren't that bad."

She shrugged, hoping the gesture hid the hurt she was feeling. "I'm used to taking care of myself. I can do this."

But if she didn't get moving she would be flat on her butt in about ten seconds.

"Tomorrow—" he scooped her into his arms "—not tonight. Time to get you into your jammies and into bed."

Cradled against his strong, wide chest, she struggled to breathe. Her muscles tensed. Her senses reeled.

What was happening to her?

Sarah wanted to be strong, but she also wanted to collapse against him and forget everything in the past and what would happen in the future. But she couldn't. Not when the feel of his heartbeat sent hers into a frenetic rhythm. Or when the musky scent of him made her want to take another sniff.

"You don't have to do this." She tried to keep the panic out of her voice. "I'm okay."

Or would be once she was out of his arms and into bed.

Alone.

With the door locked.

Sarah's gaze locked on his lips. Heat exploded inside her. She looked away.

"You're not okay." He carried her down the hallway. "It doesn't take a medical degree to see you're exhausted."

She opened her mouth to deny it, but couldn't. "I'll feel better in the morning."

"I'd rather you feel better now."

Maybe if she had a good cry or if he kissed her...

He kicked open the bathroom door with his foot and flipped on the light with his elbow. He set her on her feet in the bathroom, keeping his hands on her. "Let's get you ready for bed."

Her heart beat a rapid tattoo. She leaned against the sink counter for support. "My toiletry kit is in my suitcase."

A coworker had packed a bag for Sarah and driven it to the hospital yesterday.

Cullen opened a drawer and pulled out a new toothbrush. He unwrapped the plastic covering. "Use this."

"You have spare toothbrushes?"

"People sack out here if they don't want to drive home."

People? Or women? Sarah didn't want to know.

He squirted toothpaste on it. "Here you go."

She took the toothbrush. One minute he seemed upset at her, the next he was concerned. The flip-flopping made her dizzy. Or maybe it was the pain medication. That could explain her crying.

"I'll brush your teeth for you," he said.

She shoved the toothbrush into her mouth. "Got it."

"Be right back."

Sarah took advantage of the moment of privacy. Then after brushing her teeth, she washed her face and combed the tangles out of her hair. The effort wiped her out. She released a frustrated breath.

Cullen stood in the doorway. "Finished?"

Sarah nodded. He followed her to the guest room.

A queen-size bed with a headboard made of twigs dominated the room. He'd straightened the bedding and pulled back the covers for her, something he'd done for her when he worked graveyard shifts. Her chest tightened with memories and regrets.

A full glass of water sat on the knotty-pine nightstand. A cookie lay on a paper towel. Tears returned to her eyes. "I don't deserve—"

He placed his finger at her lips. "Shhh."

The slight touch sent chills down her spine. She couldn't have said anything if she'd wanted to.

Cullen tucked a strand of hair behind her ear. "I didn't take good care of you earlier."

Her heart stilled. She knew he meant today, but a part of her wished he'd meant during their marriage.

"I'm making up for this afternoon," he continued.

Sarah released the breath she hadn't realized she was holding. Her disappointment was a not-so-subtle reminder of how stupid she became around Cullen. "You're not my manservant."

Mischief did the tango in his eyes. "I could be if that's what you want."

She wanted...him.

No, that was the pain medication talking. More tears filled her eyes. She wiped her face with the back of her hand.

He embraced her. "It's going to be okay."

Not with her breasts pressed against his broad, muscular chest and her heart thudding in her chest. "I'm sorry. I'm all loopy."

"You're cute when you're all loopy."

He pulled her closer and she sank against him, too tired to keep fighting herself. He felt so good. Warm. And strong. "You're cute when I'm all loopy."

Cullen laughed. The deep sound was the best medicine of all. "Where are your pajamas?"

"In my suitcase."

"Sit."

She sat on the bed while he opened her suitcase.
He removed a floral-print nightshirt. "This work?"

"Yes."

Cullen placed the nightie on the bed. He pulled
on her bra band through her T-shirt. The strap un-
hooked.

Heat rushed up her neck. "You've, um, always
been good at that."

"A little rusty, but it's like riding a bike."

Her pulse quickened. "I haven't ridden in a while."

Too long. She missed it. Missed him. No, she
missed the idea of him, of what they could have
had together if fairy tales existed. This—what was
happening right now—wasn't real.

He brushed his hand over her hair. "You can always hop back on."

Sarah's mouth went dry. She opened her mouth to
speak, but no words came out.

"Let's get your shirt off you."

Let's not. She crossed her arm and her cast in front
of her chest. "I want to see if I can do it."

"Sure."

She waited for him to turn around. He didn't. Frustration grew. "Maybe you could face the other way."

He turned to the wall.

Self-preservation helped her undress and put on the nightshirt. Thank goodness she'd taken the pain pills, or she'd be really hurting. "You can turn around."

"I'm impressed."

She was about to fall asleep. "Thanks."

"Time for bed."

Before Sarah could blink, she was horizontal with her head against the pillow. She had no idea how he'd managed to get her in this position so effortlessly, but she was beyond the point of caring.

Cullen arranged the sheet and comforter over her.

"You don't have to do this," she said quietly.

He brushed his lips across her forehead with a kiss as light as a feather. "It's been a long day, an even longer week. The least I can do is tuck you in."

Emotion overflowed from her heart. She felt so special.

"Sweet dreams, Lavagirl," he said.

Who needed dreams? Reality was pretty sweet right now. Sarah wanted him to stay, to hold her, until she fell asleep.

"Thank you, Dr. Gray." She felt dreamy and a tad wistful. "For everything."

"I'm right across the hall if you need anything."

He turned off the light, walked out of the room and closed the door behind him.

And then it hit her.

She and Cullen had never spent a night in the same place without sleeping in the same bed. Not until to-night. Her heart panged.

A door closed out in the hallway. She heard water. The shower.

Well, there was always a first time. Sarah touched the empty space next to her. But she had to admit she'd rather there wasn't.

Even if she knew better.

CHAPTER SIX

SOMEONE COUGHED. CULLEN bolted upright from a dead sleep. He blinked, not quite sure what was going on. Rays of sunlight peeked into the room around the edges of the window blinds. The digital clock on his nightstand read 6:45 a.m. Another cough.

Sarah.

Pulse pounding, he jumped out of bed, ran to her room and flung open the door. She lay in bed. Her hair was a tangled mess. Her face, what he could see through her hair, was pale. "Sarah?"

"I coughed." Her voice sounded hoarse. "It hurt."

"I'm sure it did." He sat next to her. "Let me check your incision."

Her eyes widened with a hint of panic. "It was the cough."

He brushed the hair away from her face. His fingers touched her cheek. She didn't feel warm. "I want to make sure."

She pulled the blanket to her neck. "You don't have to go to all this trouble."

"It's no trouble." He understood Sarah's leeriness. In spite of being a little out of it last night, she must have realized he'd been turned on. Even after a cold shower, he'd wanted to sleep in here, to hold her, to breathe in her scent. Loneliness did strange things to a man. "If you were in a SNF, someone would check you."

"Yes, but not..."

"Me."

She nodded. "I'm sorry."

"Don't apologize."

Her fingers rubbed the edge of the blanket. She wouldn't meet his eyes. "It's the situation. I'm not sure how to feel around you. Parts of last night were nice, then awkward, then nice again. So nice I hated sleeping alone."

A combination of relief and satisfaction radiated through him. He'd thought the same thing. He touched her shoulder.

Her muscles tensed beneath his hand.

"I get it," he admitted. "Having you here is..."

"Weird."

"Different," he said at the same time. "A little weird, too."

She blew out a puff of air. "Good. I mean, not that things are weird, but that I'm not alone or imagining things."

"You're not alone." He'd been imagining things about her all night. Unfortunately. Because those fantasies would never become reality. "We're adults. We can handle this."

"It's not like we have another choice."

If only… "It is what it is until you're ready to go back to Bellingham."

"If things get too weird we can talk it out."

She had wanted to talk about everything. He hated doing that. He'd been talked out after his parents had the family attend counseling and grief sessions following Blaine's death. The intense sessions helped, but they also frustrated Cullen because no amount of counseling or rehab had been able to help his brother kick his drug addiction.

Sarah looked expectantly at him.

"Sure, we can talk." He relented. "May I check your incision?"

She lowered the blanket. "It's not like you haven't seen this before."

He slowly raised the hem of her nightshirt over her thighs. The bruises were fading. He lifted the material higher, past her orange polka-dotted bikini panties that showed off the curve of her hip. He willed his hand not to tremble. He continued to the large incision on her abdomen from her emergency splenectomy.

Cullen might have seen her body before, but he liked seeing all that creamy skin again. His gaze strayed back to her panties. He swallowed.

Focus.

The skin around the sutures wasn't any more red then it had been at the hospital. No drainage, either. He placed his fingertips on her stomach. The skin wasn't hot, but boy did she feel nice. Soft, smooth, silky.

He dragged his hand away. "No drainage or rash. Are you hungry?"

She nodded.

"That's a good sign." He pulled down the hem of her nightshirt before he became more unprofessional. "Has the pain lessened since the surgery?"

"Yes, until I coughed."

"Next time you have to cough place a pillow over your incision." He stood. "Let's get you up and moving. That should ease some of the pain."

She scrunched her nose. "It's too early for you to be up if you have to work tonight."

Her concern brought a smile to his face. "I'll take a nap later."

"You're sure?"

"Positive." He cupped her elbow and helped her out of bed. "Is it hard to breathe?"

"Nope."

"Let's see how you feel walking."

She moved slowly and carefully, the way she should to make sure she didn't fall. "It helps."

He noticed her long legs, liked the curve of her calf, the slender slope of her ankles. "You're doing great."

She walked out of the bedroom. "I must look pretty frightening."

"Not frightening." He followed her down the hall. "You look pretty good for someone recovering from a bad fall, broken bones and surgery."

She glanced over her shoulder, her green eyes hopeful. "Any chance I could shower?"

An image of him taking off her panties flashed in his mind. He gave his head a mental shake. "Uh, sure. I'll have to wrap your cast."

"That's what the nurse did at the hospital," Sarah said with a relieved smile. "I may need you to pour the shampoo into my left hand."

Or he could join her in the shower and wash her hair for her. He wouldn't mind lathering her up.

Strike that. Cullen pushed the idea from his head. He found it too easy to think about her as his wife, not his soon-to-be ex-wife. She'd wanted out of the marriage. No reason to assume she wanted back in. Not that he wanted her back. He didn't. At least most of the time, he didn't. "Let's get you fed, then cleaned up."

* * *

Sarah stood in the bathroom wearing her orange robe and nothing underneath. She stared at the tile floor, not wanting to meet Cullen's watchful eyes. She tightened the belt around her waist as best she could with one hand so the robe wouldn't slip open.

His height and wide shoulders made the space feel cramped even though the bathroom was larger than the one at the hospital. He checked the plastic around her cast. "It should stay dry."

"I don't think any water is going to come close to my cast."

He turned on the shower. Water splashed against the tub and curtain. "That's the plan."

Cullen had always been a planner. Too bad he hadn't stuck to his plans instead of letting her derail them. That would have saved them both a lot of heartache. Well, at least her. "Have your life figured out again?"

His gaze met hers. "Pretty much. I made a few changes."

Like removing her from his future plans. She pinched the bridge of her nose, ignoring the hollow feeling inside her.

He checked the water temperature. "Ready?"
Not really. "Sure."
He pulled back the shower curtain. "There's a mat

on the bottom of the tub, so you shouldn't slip, but be careful."

"Okay."

She waited for him to leave. He didn't.

"Aren't you getting in?" he asked.

Cullen stared at her as if she had something on her face. Leftover French toast, perhaps? She rubbed the back of her hand over her mouth. "Are you staying in here?"

"Yes."

It was as simple and as complicated as that.

"I need to hand you shampoo," he reminded her.

Oh, yeah. She'd forgotten about that. But still she hesitated. "This is kind of awkward."

"Only if we make it awkward."

"I'm not trying to."

"Neither am I."

"But I'm the one who is naked under my robe."

"I can undress."

She gave him a look.

He grinned, then faced the door. "Better?"

"Yes, thank you." Mustering her courage with a deep breath wasn't going to work, with her incision and ribs. She settled for a slight intake of air, untied the belt, dropped her robe and stepped inside the tub. She closed the shower curtain. "You can turn around now."

"Is the water the right temperature?"

Hot water poured over her. Steam rose toward the ceiling. She picked up a bar of soap. "Perfect."

"I remember you like it hot."

She remembered the showers they'd taken together. Hot water pulsating down on them. Washing each other. Kissing. Touching.

The soap slipped out of her hand and clattered to the tub.

"Sarah—"

"I dropped the soap," she said at the same time.

"Can you reach it?" he asked.

Bending hurt. But she wasn't about to ask him to get it for her. That would be too awkward. Too… tempting. "No, but it's okay. I really just wanted to wash my hair."

"I've got the shampoo," he said. "Stick out your hand when you want some."

Once her hair was wet enough, she extended her left arm. The cooler air temperature made her shiver. Goose bumps covered her exposed skin.

He poured a dollop of shampoo onto her palm. "Is that enough?"

"Yes."

Washing her hair was easier this time. "I'm getting the hang of using one hand."

"Just takes time."

Time she didn't have. For the past twenty-four hours, Cullen had occupied the majority of her thoughts. Not Mount Baker. Once she had work to distract her everything would return to normal. She couldn't wait for that to happen. She rinsed the shampoo from her hair.

"Need more?" he asked.

Yes, but not from him. He hadn't been able to give her what she needed. She couldn't be the wife he wanted. That was why they were better off apart. Still, the thought made her heart hurt. Not a want-to-throw-herself-a-pity-party aching, but a too-bad-this-couldn't-have-worked pining. "I'm good."

At least when it came to shampoo.

After she returned to the institute with her marriage and Cullen behind her, everything in her life would be good, too. Given how bad things had been, it sure couldn't get any worse.

Later that evening, the doorbell rang. Sarah remained on the couch while Cullen answered the door. Her babysitter for the night, Leanne Thomas, must have arrived.

Sarah was looking forward to Cullen going to work. A physical separation from him would be a relief, even though she'd spent most of her day in bed while he caught up on things around the cabin.

But she'd been thinking about him constantly. On her mind was the last place he belonged. Well, actually her heart was the last place, but that wasn't going to happen again.

A pretty woman with long, shiny brown hair, an easy smile and wearing a huge diamond engagement ring carried in a platter of mini red velvet cupcakes. She placed the dessert on the kitchen table, then removed a green tote bag from her shoulder. "Hi, I'm Leanne."

"I'm Sarah." Cullen had called the by-the-book paramedic and mountain-rescue volunteer tough as nails, but Sarah didn't get that impression at all. "Nice to meet you."

"The pleasure is mine." Leanne glanced at Cullen, who was sticking a water bottle into his backpack. "Hope I'm not late."

"Right on time." He swung a backpack strap over his right shoulder. "Thanks for taking the overnight shift. I left a list of instructions on the breakfast bar. Sarah's meds are on the kitchen counter. She should rest as much as possible. Short walks are okay, but not outside."

"Bummer. I thought I could take her on a midnight stroll around Mirror Lake," Leanne teased.

His gaze hardened. "You're kidding."

Sarah shook her head. He needed to lighten up and not take things so seriously.

Leanne's mouth quirked. "Give me a little credit."

"Just making sure," he said. "Call me if you have any questions."

What? Sarah bit her lower lip. He hadn't wanted her to call him at work no matter what was going on. If she did contact him, he never got back to her. Most of the times she'd tried calling had been because she missed him and wanted to hear his voice.

"I'm sure Sarah will be able to answer any questions I might have," Leanne said.

"Definitely." Sarah liked how direct Leanne was. "I don't know what instructions Cullen left, but my doctor's orders are to take my medication. Sleep. Rest. Sleep some more. Rest some more."

Leanne frowned. "Sounds boring."

"It is," Sarah agreed. "I fear I'm turning into a couch potato."

Cullen's lip curled. "Resting is important if you want to recover."

"True, but you can still do stuff while you take it easy," Leanne said. "I'll have to see what I can come up with."

"Thomas," Cullen said, his voice containing a clear warning.

"Relax," Leanne countered in a stern voice that

made Sarah bite back a giggle. "Sarah will be fine. Get going before we throw you out."

He raised his hands in mock surrender. "I'm going."

As soon as the door closed, Leanne sat on the couch. "I'm sorry about your fall."

"Thanks. I was at the wrong place, wrong time."

"Well, you're in the right place now. Hood Hamlet will be good for you. It won't be long until you're exploring Main Street."

"I can't wait."

Colorful prisms of light reflected off Leanne's diamond ring and danced around the living room. She stared lovingly at her ring.

"Congrats on your engagement," Sarah said.

Leanne beamed. "Thanks. I still can't believe I'm getting married."

"Have you set a wedding date?"

She nodded. "The Saturday before Christmas. We hadn't been together long when my fiancé, Christian, proposed on Christmas Day so we thought a year engagement sounded good."

Very good. A year was long enough to get know someone, but not so long you would feel you'd wasted a lot of time if it didn't work out. "Cullen said you're a member of OMSAR. Does Christian belong, too?"

"No. He climbs and thought about joining, but he

thinks I need something of my own, since we work together."

"Smart guy."

A dreamy expression filled Leanne's brown eyes. "Very smart and smokin' hot. Ever since we got together I feel like I won the lottery."

"I know that feeling."

"With Doc?"

Cullen had treated her with such respect from the moment they met. No other man in her life had ever done that. The cascade of memories made it hard to breathe. How had it gone so wrong? She nodded.

"How did you meet?" Leanne asked.

"I was attending the Red Rocks Rendezvous. We both lived in Seattle at the time and a mutual climbing acquaintance introduced us. A few hours later we ended up in the same self-rescue clinic."

"Sounds like fate."

"Only if fate has a really bad sense of humor."

Leanne's brow wrinkled. "Doc mentioned you're getting a divorce."

Sarah ignored the pang in her heart. "Yes."

"I've gotten to know Doc pretty well the past few months," Leanne said. "At first I thought he took himself way too seriously and had a stick up his butt. But he's a good guy."

"Cullen is a great guy. Not many men would bring their future ex-wives home to care for them."

"This is none of my business, but I'm still going to ask." Warmth and concern sounded in Leanne's voice. "Is there a possibility the two of you will reconcile?

Sarah's heart thudded. Her biggest fear was allowing him to get close to her again. "No chance. We eloped in Las Vegas two days after we met. It was impulsive and romantic. The first few months were like living in paradise. But we shouldn't have jumped into marriage without getting to know each other better."

Oh, no. She touched her mouth. She'd said way too much.

Compassion filled Leanne's eyes. "Love knows no logic."

Neither does lust. Sarah kept telling herself what she'd felt for Cullen was lust not love. She'd been too afraid to let him fully inside her heart, afraid he would leave her like everyone else in her life had. But what they'd shared had been nice—at times, wonderful—while it lasted. She only wished it could have lasted a little while longer.

Like forever.

The next morning Cullen unlocked the cabin's front door. He yawned wide enough for a hummingbird to fit inside. His restless nights had caught up with him. He had one thought on his brain—sleep. He'd considered pulling off the road and taking a catnap, but he didn't want to keep Leanne. He also wanted to see how Sarah was doing. He'd pulled out his cell phone more than once during his shift, but he hadn't wanted to wake them.

He stepped into the cabin. The scent of freshly brewed coffee and something baking made his mouth water. He wasn't used to coming home to such pleasant smells. Caffeine would mess with his sleep, but his stomach growled for whatever was cooking.

Feminine laughter filled the air—something Cullen had missed hearing. Sarah's laugh seeped into him, filling up all the empty places inside with soothing warmth. He might have a great place to live in a wonderful town with a supportive community, but something was missing from his life—a woman.

After the divorce things will be better.

His mantra didn't make him feel quite as good as it had a couple of weeks ago.

In the living room he saw the backs of Sarah's and Leanne's heads. They sat on the couch.

"Good morning, ladies," he said.

Leanne turned and greeted him with a wide smile. "Hey, Doc. Just in time. The muffins will be ready in a few minutes."

Sarah looked at him. No smile. No excitement in her eyes. Nothing.

He would have appreciated some reaction from her. Maybe she was tired. Or hurting. But he hoped not.

"Busy shift?" Sarah asked.

Cardiac arrests, fractures, appendicitis, a gunshot victim and two car accidents. Not to mention earaches, asthma attacks, fevers and cuts. "Typical."

"That'll change next week," Leanne said. "Full moon."

"Thanks for the warning." He noticed the two were looking at a magazine. "How did things go?"

"Fine," Sarah said. "I went to bed a half hour after Leanne arrived and woke up an hour ago."

"Easiest gig I've ever had. Sarah is the perfect patient." Leanne held up a thick bridal magazine full of glossy photographs. "She also has great wedding-planning advice."

"Wedding planning, huh?" That surprised Cullen. "I suppose Sarah knows all about being married by an Elvis impersonator."

Leanne's mouth formed a perfect O. She looked at Sarah. "You didn't tell me that."

She shrugged. "I figured getting married in Vegas implied an Elvis impersonator."

"He had that jiggling-leg thing going on." Cullen demonstrated. "'Darlin', do you take this man...'"

Leanne laughed. "Where is my cell phone? No one will believe this. You *sound* like Elvis."

Sarah nodded. "We bought a wedding package that included a video of the ceremony. Each time I watch it, I'm amazed how well Cullen has nailed the voice."

His heart kicked in his chest. "You still watch the video?"

Sarah's gaze flew to the magazine. "I used to. It's packed away in a box somewhere."

Cullen hadn't expected she'd kept the video. He was sure she'd destroyed all evidence of their wedding. He wouldn't have been surprised if she'd gone so far as to toss her wedding ring into the garbage. He'd thought about getting rid of his, but he'd decided to wait for the divorce to be finalized.

The oven timer buzzed.

Leanne stood, walked to the kitchen and removed a muffin tin from the oven. "I hope you like blueberry."

A tight smiled formed on Sarah's lips. "I love them. So does Cullen."

He remembered lazy mornings when he wasn't working. Sleeping in, having sex, taking long showers together, going to the corner coffee shop to pick up coffee and muffins.

Leanne put the muffins on a dinner plate and carried them to the living room with salad plates, napkins, a butter knife and butter.

"If you don't mind, I'm going to take off." She placed everything on the coffee table. "Christian is finished with his shift. We only have one day off the same since the chief put us on different squads."

"Go have fun," Sarah said. "Thanks for staying with me and making muffins."

"Happy to help out. I'll be back when it's my turn." Leanne grabbed her tote bag. "Be sure to go through the magazine and see what else you come up with."

"Will do," Sarah said.

"I'll walk you out," Cullen said.

Leanne fell in step next to him. "Ever the gentleman."

He opened the door and followed her outside.

"I'd been wondering why you haven't been dating," Leanne said.

"I figured it would be better to wait until the divorce was official."

"When will that be?" she asked.

"My attorney knows Sarah is staying with me. He thinks everything can be settled shortly."

"Sarah's great." Leanne pursed her lips. "You're sure a divorce is what you want?"

"Positive. Sarah wants one, too, so don't get any ideas. Half the town has tried setting me up on blind dates. I don't need them interfering in my estranged marriage."

Leanne held up her hands. "Just asking. And since Sarah's staying with you, you're not quite as estranged as you were."

"Thomas."

A knowing grin lit up her face. "What?"

Cullen let it go. He knew she was only trying to help. "Thanks for staying with Sarah."

"You're welcome," she said. "See you soon."

He went back inside to find Sarah looking at the bridal magazine. The muffins sat untouched. "Aren't you going to eat?"

She closed the magazine. "I was waiting for you."

That was polite. He sat next to her. "Do you want me to butter yours?"

"Thanks, but I've got it." Sarah placed a muffin on a plate. She awkwardly sliced the top then added a pat of butter. "These smell so good."

Cullen took one. "Leanne's got a thing for muffins and chocolate."

Sarah rested her plate on her lap. "She's nice. I like her."

"I thought you might," he said. "Leanne reminds me of you."

"I'm nothing like her."

"You both work in male-dominated environments. You're competent and intelligent. You ski and climb."

"Okay, I see the commonality." Sarah bit into the muffin. "But I wish I cooked as well as she does."

"Yeah, that would be nice."

She swatted his arm. "I'm not that bad."

"I'm joking. You're a good cook." He noticed the bridal magazine on her lap. "I'm curious how you know so much about wedding planning, when we eloped."

She wiped her mouth with a napkin. "I told you I was engaged."

"I assumed it was a short engagement."

"Two and a half years."

He drew back. "That's a long time."

"Longer when you add in the years we dated."

"When was this?"

"Four years before I met you."

He did a quick calculation. "You must have been really young when you met him."

"Too young. And stupid," she admitted. "But I thought I knew better."

"Why didn't you tell me?" he asked.

"You and I got married two days after we met. I figured it didn't matter."

He set his half-eaten muffin on his plate. "What happened?"

She stared at the magazine. "Dylan entered my life at a time I felt very alone. I thought I was so lucky he wanted to be with me. There were some red flags, but I charged ahead with wedding plans. That morning..."

Cullen leaned toward her, feeling as if a cornice of snow had collapsed on top of him. "The morning of your wedding day?"

She nodded. "I was in a small room at the back of the church. I'd worked two jobs to buy my wedding gown and pay for the reception. I was fixing my veil when Dylan entered. He said he'd been up all night thinking about things, about us, and had come to a conclusion. He couldn't marry me. The wedding was off."

Anger surged at how badly Sarah must have been hurt. Cullen balled his hands. "What a loser."

She shrugged. "He said I wasn't anything special. I would have held him back. I don't blame him for not wanting to marry me."

"Don't say that. The guy had some serious issues if he thought any of those things about you."

"Yeah, issues with me." If Sarah was trying to sound lighthearted, she hadn't succeeded and that bothered Cullen even more. "But I got over him. Moved on. Met you."

The conversation they'd had outside the wedding chapel in Las Vegas rushed back.

Why don't we go inside and make things official? If we elope, you won't forget about me when we get back to Seattle or leave me standing at the altar after we've dated for years and I've planned a spectacular wedding for us.

Cullen remembered his reply.

I would never leave you like that.

Guilt lodged in his throat. He *had* left her. The minute she mentioned divorce he'd hightailed it out of the apartment. Had mentioning divorce been a test? To see how committed he was? Part of him wanted to be angry if she'd been testing without his knowing it, yet…even if she hadn't been doing that, he'd failed. He'd run the second he had a chance. No wonder she'd freaked out on him whenever he tried to contact her about the divorce. "I'm sorry."

"No apologies needed. Getting jilted happened way before you."

"I know, but I left you, too. If I'd known…"

"Would it have changed anything?" she asked.

He thought long and hard. Things hadn't been going well between them. She'd been pulling away from him. He hadn't like how out of control he felt around her. "Probably not."

Sarah's lip quivered. "I appreciate your honesty."

"I appreciate your telling me about this."

A marble statue had a warmer smile than hers. "Better late than never."

Except it was too late to do anything about it now. Or was it?

CHAPTER SEVEN

WOULD IT HAVE changed anything?

Probably not.

Cullen's two words reaffirmed Sarah's actions of a year ago. He'd even apologized. Something she'd never expected him to do. She should feel relieved she'd been spot-on about their relationship. Marriage had never tied them to each other as a couple, as husband and wife. Instead of relief, a heavy sadness bore down on her. She leaned back on the couch, looking at the wood-beamed ceiling.

"Need a refill?" Cullen asked from the kitchen.

"No, thanks." She flexed her left hand to stop it from shaking. "My cup is full."

She'd known things were over between them. She was used to the heartache and resentment over her failed marriage, so she wasn't sure why what Cullen had said bothered her so much.

Face it. Some people weren't cut out for marriage. Like her. Her parents. Must be something in the DNA.

She glanced at the cover of the bridal magazine.

The beautiful model dressed in a couture gown with perfectly applied makeup and coiffed hair glowed with a radiance Sarah envied. The woman wasn't a bride, but more thought had gone into the carefully executed photo shoot than into their eloping.

Her appetite disappeared.

Cullen returned to the living room with a steaming cup of coffee. "You look better today."

"I'm getting there." Physically, at least. Emotionally was another story. She rubbed her thumb against her fingertips. "You must be tired after working all night. Go to bed. I'll be fine while you sleep."

He raised his cup of coffee. "I got my second wind."

Maybe she should take a nap and give them a break from each other. She nearly laughed. Running off was Cullen's typical avoidance tactic, not hers.

"What's so funny?" he asked.

He'd been honest before. It was her turn. She met his gaze. "I'm surprised you're still here."

He sipped his coffee. "Where would I go?"

"Anywhere I'm not."

"That's—"

"What you used to do," she interrupted. "Whenever things were really good between us or when we'd disagree, you always disappeared to the hospital, some mountain-rescue thing, wherever else you could go."

He tugged at his polo-shirt collar. "I only did what I needed to do."

"Exactly."

She had never entered into the equation. It was almost as if he were different people. The Doctor. The Mountain Rescuer. The Lover. The Husband was the one role he hadn't seemed to embrace.

"I don't want to argue," he said.

"We're not arguing," she countered. "We're having a discussion."

He took a sip of his coffee. "Let's take a short walk outside instead."

She drummed her fingers on the sofa arm. "You're doing it again."

"Doing what?"

"Running away."

"I invited you on a walk."

"You're trying to change the subject because you don't want to talk."

"All you want to do is talk, even when there's nothing to discuss."

Ouch. His words stung. "I'll shut up, then."

"That's not..." He dragged his hand through his hair. "Let's go for a walk. I don't want us to fight."

"This isn't anywhere close to fighting," she explained. "Sometimes when my parents fought, the police got involved. One of my stepfathers burned our clothes in the front yard. And my ex-fiancé…"

"Did he hurt you?"

"Not physically. But Dylan's words could be as powerful as a fist."

Cullen reached for her.

She moved away from him. His compassion and tenderness were not what she needed right now. "I'm not proud I allowed it to happen for as long as it did or wasn't the one to break up, but at least I knew where I stood with him."

"You know how I feel…felt about you. There's no reason to bring this up now." He stood. "I'm going for a walk. If you'd rather stay inside…"

"No." The word spewed from her mouth like lava out of Mount Etna. "I want to go outside."

"Then let's go."

Five minutes later she found herself standing on Cullen's driveway in her boots and wearing a jacket. The sharp scent of pine wafted on the breeze. Sunlight kissed her cheeks. She breathed in, filling her lungs with the crisp mountain air.

"Isn't this better than arguing inside?" Cullen asked.

"It's nice, but the inside wasn't so bad," she said. "The best part of disagreeing is making up."

"I don't think so."

"That's because you never stuck around for the make-up sex."

Cullen started to speak, then pressed his lips together.

Humming a little tune, Sarah walked away from him. For the first time in a long while, she had the upper hand. She wanted to savor the moment.

Leaves and twigs crunched under her feet. She walked along the edge of the road.

He caught up to her. "So, is there a statute of limitation on make-up sex?"

Sarah froze. That was…unexpected. She looked over at him.

Wicked laughter lit his eyes. "Seems I missed out."

She raised her chin. "Your loss."

His charming smile unleashed a colony of bats in her stomach. "Yours, too."

Darn him. This was what he always did. Turn off the serious side. Get all sexy and fun and flirty. Make her insides hot and gooey. He hadn't changed one bit.

She casually lifted one shoulder, but her heart pounded like a jackhammer. "You win some. You lose some."

He stepped closer to her. Too close for anything other than kissing her.

He wouldn't, would he? She gulped, not sure what

she wanted the answer to be. Okay, she knew. But *yes* wasn't the correct response if she wanted to play it safe.

He cocked a brow. "So the statute…"

It was up to her. Temptation flared, only to be tempered by common sense. What she wanted warred with what she needed, but self-preservation reigned supreme.

Her fingernails dug into her palms. "Expired."

Sarah marched down the road as if her life depended on putting distance between them. Her abdomen ached. She kept going. She didn't know where she was going. She didn't care.

Cullen grabbed her hand. "Slow down. You'll hurt yourself."

"I'm fine."

"No, you're not. You're mad at me. Even madder than you were inside."

She pursed her lips. She wasn't about to give him the satisfaction of being right.

"I know this because you have a crease between your eyebrows."

Sarah touched the spot.

He moved her finger. "Right here."

She felt the line, but still wasn't going to admit it.

Cullen glanced to his right. His eyes widened. "Look."

Sarah had no idea what he wanted her to see. "What?"

"Shhh." Cullen touched her lips with his finger, then positioned himself behind her. His chest pressed against her back. He brought his left arm around her and pointed. "A doe and two fawns."

Awareness hummed through Sarah. He emanated heat and strength. Her pulse raced.

She couldn't focus. Bigfoot could have been standing in front of her and she wouldn't have noticed him.

Her reaction made zero sense. She was still angry, resentful and hurt over their breakup. Their marriage was over. Yet her body didn't seem to understand that.

"See them?" he whispered.

The warmth of his breath against her neck gave her chills. Her gaze followed the length of his arm until she saw the deer. A momma and her two babies, munching on a bush. Her breath stilled. "So cute."

"I've seen these three around the cabin," he said quietly.

The deer ate without glancing at them. The fawns were more interested in keeping an eye on their mother, who paid close attention to both of them.

Sarah wished her mom had cared as much for her. Wished Cullen had, too. She shoved her left hand into her jacket pocket. "I haven't noticed them or any others."

"You will. You haven't been here long."

It felt as if she'd been here forever. "I'll be on the lookout."

The doe stiffened. She looked in their direction, then past them, as if she sensed something.

A car drove down the road. The sound of the engine splintered the silence.

The deer bounded into the trees, her two fawns following.

If only Sarah could go back to Bellingham. She wanted to pretend none of this had happened—her accident and her injuries and her reaction to Cullen. She wanted it to all go away.

He faced her. "They'll be back."

What she and Cullen had shared once would never return. A sigh welled up inside her. She parted her lips.

He lowered his head to hers and kissed her.

Sarah's heart stalled.

His kiss was gentle and sweet. He didn't touch her except with his lips. But that was enough.

Her nerve endings stirred to life as if awakened from a deep slumber. Pleasurable sensations pulsed through her. She'd forgotten how wonderful his kiss was.

He backed away from her.

Sarah took a step back herself. Swallowed. "Why did you do that?"

"Make-up kiss."

She laughed.

"The statute of limitations for a make-up kiss has to be longer than for make-up sex," he said.

"If it isn't, I doubt I'll press charges."

He grinned wryly. "That's generous of you, Lava-girl."

Her lips tingled. "Only repaying your generosity, Dr. Gray."

His smile spread, matching the heat spreading inside her. He tucked a strand of hair behind her ear.

If she weren't careful, he could overwhelm her. "But we shouldn't make kisses a habit."

"You're probably right about that," Cullen agreed. "As long as we don't argue, we should be fine."

Probably. Should be. He'd left a lot of wiggle room.

That meant it would be up to her to make sure nothing more happened. And even though Sarah knew better, she was kind of hoping there would be more kisses.

Cullen couldn't believe he'd kissed Sarah.

A momentary lapse? If that had been the case he would have kissed her with more passion. He'd been careful to keep things under control. Not easy with the images of make-up sex shuffling through his mind. But he had still enjoyed the kiss.

Had he run away, as she said?

Cullen had left a few times whenever he felt his control slipping or was too overwhelmed by her. But she had to be exaggerating the number of times, caught up in some revised history of their marriage to make her feel better, less guilty for bringing up the topic of divorce.

He peeked into her room. She was sound asleep.

Good. Cullen needed sleep himself. Caffeine was keeping him going at the moment. But he wanted to do something first. He entered his room, closed the door and made a call on his cell phone.

"Hey, Doc," OMSAR rescue leader Sean Hughes said. "How's Sarah?"

"Napping. She's looking better."

"Good to hear."

Cullen adjusted the phone at his ear. "I'm signed up for your ready team tomorrow, but I want to stay home with Sarah."

"No worries," Sean said. "We'll get it covered."

"Thanks, and I'm sorry."

"No apology necessary. Do what you have to do."

That's what Cullen was trying to do. Even though he wasn't sure why he was doing it.

* * *

A week later sunlight streamed through Sarah's bed-room window. The snow must have stopped over-night. Not that good weather would change her agenda for the day. Physical therapy and a walk were as exciting as things got. She could work on her lap-top for a few minutes, but headaches and her arm limited her productivity. Still, she forced herself out of bed and into the hallway.

The scent of freshly brewed coffee and something baking filled the air. Sarah's mouth watered at the tantalizing aromas. Her tummy grumbled.

She wondered who would be staying with her today. The delicious smells wafting in the air told her it wasn't Zoe Hughes, who was scheduled to be here. The former socialite was beautiful and friendly, but she couldn't cook. Hannah had been here yes-terday, so that left Carly or Leanne.

Unless it was…Cullen.

The thought gave Sarah an unexpected boost of energy. She quickened her pace.

She hadn't seen him in days. He'd been working his shifts and covering for other doctors. He'd ex-plained he was doing this because of being up in Seattle with her, not to get away from her now. He'd even called to say hello, something he'd never done, which Sarah appreciated.

But his absences reminded her of how she'd always been so desperate to see him when they lived together. She wasn't desperate now. She was…eager. The logic behind her eagerness couldn't readily be explained, but her frustration could be.

Sarah's slow recovery gave her insight into how magma must feel as it rose out of the earth's mantle and moved into the crust. She wasn't a mix of solids, melt and gases, but the physics behind making progress with her injuries was similar and taking way too much time.

In the hallway, Sarah noticed someone in the kitchen. Someone with brown hair. Someone female with two braids.

Not Cullen. Leanne.

Sarah stumbled, but regained her balance before she fell. She'd experienced a lifetime of disappointments, everything from forgotten birthdays to having her marriage disintegrate. Not seeing Cullen was nothing in the grand scheme of things.

Leanne greeted Sarah with a smile. "You're up early today."

"I went to bed around eight." Sarah hadn't been that tired, but she'd wanted Hannah to go home and say good-night to her three children. Being tucked in meant a lot to kids. It would have meant a lot to Sarah if her parents had done that.

Cullen must have come and gone while she was sleeping. If he'd returned home at all. A few times this week he hadn't, and not knowing where he was bugged her.

Sarah leaned against the breakfast bar. "I thought Zoe was going to be here."

"She had to run to Portland, so two of us are tag-teaming it." Leanne picked up the coffeepot. "You're stuck with me until lunchtime."

"You're the one who's stuck." These women were so kind and friendly. "I appreciate what you've been doing for me."

"It's our pleasure." The sincerity in Leanne's voice touched Sarah's heart. "This is what friends do for each other."

Cullen was so lucky. Hood Hamlet was a very special place. A perfect place for a family. Not that she would ever have one…

As Leanne poured coffee into two cups, light glimmered off her diamond engagement ring. The pretty paramedic had found her one true love at the fire station. A younger man who adored her, according to Zoe.

Sarah felt a pang. Maybe happy-ever-afters were possible for some people. She hoped so for her new friend's sake.

"Sit." Leanne placed the steaming mugs on the table. "I baked banana-nut muffins."

Sarah sat. "I like those as much as blueberry ones."

People in Hood Hamlet took care of each other and strangers like her, too. Home-cooked, healthy meals were either made or arrived each day. Though Cullen had been away so much, he'd ended up with leftovers. When he came home...

Her throat tightened. Cullen hadn't fallen right back into the same pattern of their marriage, but the longer he stayed away, the more she worried he might.

Leanne returned to the table with a platter of muffins. "Dig in."

"Thanks." Sarah bit into one. The flavors and warmth filled her mouth. "Delicious. I like the walnuts."

"Me, too."

She took another bite, but couldn't stop thinking about Cullen. Thoughts of him more than made up for his physical absence. That added to her growing frustrations over her injuries and inability to get much work done. She tore off a piece of the muffin and shoved it into her mouth.

Concern clouded Leanne's brown eyes. "Taking it easy is hard for you."

Sarah stared into her coffee cup. "It's downright aggravating."

"Cullen told me you're improving every day."

Hurt sliced through her. He hadn't told her that. She shouldn't take it personally. She wasn't his friend or a climbing and ski partner like Leanne.

So what if he'd kissed Sarah? Or spent two whole days and night taking care of her before he'd returned to a marathon of shift coverage? She was a temporary roommate and no longer a permanent part of his life—a life she was beginning to envy after a week and a half in Hood Hamlet.

Being envious was silly.

Everything she wanted and cared about was in Bellingham. Mount Baker. The institute. Her post-doc.

Leanne studied her. "Since you're doing better, maybe it's time you do something in town."

Anticipation made Sarah sit straighter. "I would love that."

"Zoe wants us to go to Taco Night at the brewpub this evening. Join us."

Sarah's stomach fluttered. "Sounds like fun, but I don't know if Cullen will agree. He can't turn off the doctor switch."

Leanne grinned. "I'll talk to him. Convince him going out will be good for you."

"He still might say no."

"Then I'll ask Paulson to help me kidnap you. He's been my best friend since I was nine. He's up for anything."

"Even kidnapping?"

"Pretty much," Leanne said. "He might draw the line at disposing of a body, but with Paulson you never know, especially if a pretty woman is involved."

A smile tugged at the corners of Sarah's lips. "Sounds like an interesting guy."

Leanne sipped her coffee. "He's a real-life Peter Pan who will never grow up, but he's also a total sweetheart. You'll meet him after lunch. He's staying with you until Cullen gets home."

Sarah perked up. "Cullen will be home tonight?"

"This afternoon. That's why tonight is perfect for you to get out."

"I'd like that." Especially if she could be with Cullen.

"It'll happen." Leanne sounded so confident.

"And if not, you and Bill can kidnap me."

A fake kidnapping sounded fun, given Sarah had been lying around since she'd arrived. Now, if she'd been lying around with Cullen...

Heat rocketed through her. Uh-oh. Better stick to

how she was going to get to Taco Night. Mexican food was as spicy as she could handle right now.

Cullen sat in the hospital cafeteria. A few crumbs from his fish and chips remained on his plate. He sipped his coffee. The caffeine would get him through the next two hours.

A good thing he needed to cover only eight hours today. He'd spent the past five days covering shifts for others and working his own. He'd ended up staying at an anesthesiologist's house rather than drive all the way home only to return a few hours later.

He missed Sarah, but enjoyed this reprieve. Being with her messed with his head. He didn't want her getting anywhere close to his heart.

But this time away from her had intensified his guilt. Not only for leaving her the way he had a year ago, but also for running away from her when they'd been living together as husband and wife. He hated admitting the truth, even to himself, but the more he thought about it, the more he realized Sarah had been correct about what he'd been doing. No wonder she'd been unhappy. After what her jerk of an ex-fiancé had done to her, Cullen must have made her feel like crap.

He never wanted to hurt her that way again. That was why he'd made it clear to her that he had shifts to make up. He had no ulterior motives in working so much this week.

And even though he wasn't with her, he thought about Sarah every day. More like several times each day. Wondered how her recovery was going; was she missing him as much as he missed her?

Curious, he called Leanne. She'd texted him this morning saying she was with Sarah instead of Zoe.

"Hey," Leanne answered. "I was going to call you."

His shoulder muscles tensed. "Sarah okay?"

"She looks better than I've seen her look all week. Stronger, too."

Relief washed over him. "Good."

"Sarah is doing so well you should bring her to Taco Night."

He hadn't been to the brewpub in three weeks. "She's not up for it."

"She wants to go," Leanne said to his surprise. "She needs to get out of the cabin."

"Sarah isn't a social butterfly. She's a scientist who would rather be on a volcano than anywhere else."

"It's not some fancy soiree. It's tacos at the brew-pub."

Everyone he knew would be there. There would be more questions. "She'll get too tired."

"I don't know how she's managed this long." Disapproval rang clear in Leanne's voice. "Just sitting around the cabin and taking short walks isn't good for her morale or her recovery."

But it was safe. He didn't have to worry about Sarah when that was all she was doing. "She does need to get out more. Next week will be better."

"Maybe for you, but not Sarah. You can stay home tonight. Paulson will bring her."

Cullen laughed. "You want Paulson to take my wife to Taco Night?"

"It's not a problem," she said. "He's with Sarah right now. The two hit it off."

Cullen's heart went splat against the cafeteria floor.

"What?" His voice rose. He lowered it. "You texted you were with her."

"This morning. I had to attend a Christmas Magic festival meeting after lunch. No worries. Paulson will take good care of Sarah."

That was what Cullen was afraid of.

CHAPTER EIGHT

BILL PAULSON SAT next to Sarah on the couch with an impish grin on his lips and a suggestive gleam in his eyes. "So what do you want to do now?"

Charming might describe Hood Hamlet, but it didn't come close to describing the friendly, easy-on-the-eyes firefighter in well-worn jeans and a faded T-shirt. Sarah enjoyed being with him. He made her feel feminine and pretty even when she looked like a boxer, albeit one who'd been out of the ring for a couple of weeks.

"I have no idea," she admitted.

The guy had a great sense of humor. He could give any pop-star pretty boy a run for the money in the looks department and kick their butts with his athletic build. He was fun to hang out with, albeit a little immature with some of his not-so-subtle, yet humorous innuendos.

"You've kept me entertained all afternoon. I'm not sure what's left for us to do," she added.

Mischief twinkled in his eyes. "I'm sure I can think of a few things."

Bill Paulson would be considered a catch, except for two things—the guy knew he was good-looking and he was an incorrigible flirt. No way would she encourage him.

He rubbed his chin. "I could paint your toenails. That has to be tough to do with your dominant hand in a cast."

Okay, the guy was a good listener. He'd taken their earlier discussion on being right-handed and come up with this. But however tempting that might sound, she could survive without nail polish. The only man who should be doing any toenail painting on her was Cullen. Not that he would. Or that she would ask him. "Thanks, but I think a nap would be better."

He scrambled off the couch. "I'll fluff your pillows. Be right back."

Sarah bit back a laugh at his eagerness to help. Bill was half player, half Boy Scout rolled into one. Adorable, but a handful if you were a single woman who happened to be attracted to him. Neither of which she was.

The front door opened. Leanne must be back.

Sarah turned to say hello, but the word died on her lips.

Cullen stormed inside, wearing his scrubs. His gaze was intense and focused on her. Lines bracketed his mouth.

"The bed's ready," Bill announced from the hallway.

Cullen's face reddened. A muscle pulsed at his jaw.

Bill grinned. "Hey, Doc. I've been taking good care of Sarah."

Cullen balled his fingers. He looked as if he wanted to punch someone. "I'll bet you have."

Sarah had never seen him act like this. She didn't like it. "Cullen?"

He glared at Bill. "What's this about a bed being ready?"

Bill held up his hands in front of him, as if to surrender. "Dude, I don't know what's got into you, but if you're thinking I'd put the moves on your pretty wife you're way off. I just fluffed her pillows."

Cullen's dark gaze bounced from Bill to her. "You fluffed her what?"

"Her pillows," Bill said.

"The pillows on my bed," Sarah clarified. "I wanted to nap."

"A nap," Cullen repeated.

"A nap," Bill reaffirmed.

Cullen seemed to be digesting the information. She didn't know what his problem was. She looked up at Bill. "You've been a big help this afternoon."

"Anytime." He smiled. "If you need a ride to Taco Night…"

"I'm taking her," Cullen said. "After her nap."

Bill pulled out his car keys from his jeans pocket. A grin twitched at his lips. "Looks like my work here is done."

"Thanks for the brownies," she said.

"You made her brownies?" Cullen asked incredulously.

"I made both of you brownies. Well, my mom did." Bill had explained how his mom cooked his meals, cleaned his house and did his washing. No wonder the guy hadn't grown up yet. He didn't need to. "She dropped them off at my place this morning."

Sarah stood. "Thank your mom for us. And thanks for keeping me company."

"My pleasure." Bill looked at Cullen. "Your wife is quite the card shark. She kicked my butt at Texas hold 'em. A good thing we weren't playing strip poker, or I'd have been buck naked in no time."

A confused expression formed on Cullen's face.

Bill didn't seem to care. Or maybe he didn't notice, since he was looking at her. "See you at the brewpub. If Doc changes his mind about going, give me a call."

With that, Bill left.

Cullen stood next to the breakfast bar. His lips narrowed. "Please tell me you know better than to get involved with a guy like Paulson."

Defensiveness rose. "Get involved? What are you talking about?"

"A lot of women like him."

Sarah didn't like Cullen's tone. "Bill's a nice guy."

"He's a total player who will never grow up."

She saw that. She didn't need Cullen pointing it out. "You're jealous."

"No, I'm not," he said with a dismissive air.

"Then why did you storm into the house like a bull from the streets of Pamplona looking for a fight?"

He took a deep breath and another, as if reining himself in yet again. "I was worried."

"Worried."

"I like Paulson," Cullen admitted. "But he'll hit on any female with a pretty smile."

"You thought he would hit on me."

He clenched his teeth. "You deserve better."

Sarah had deserved better from him, too. She raised her chin. "Yes, I do. Bill is a big flirt, but it was innocent, all in fun."

"He didn't—"

"He was a perfect gentleman."

Cullen's brow furrowed. "*Gentleman* and *Paulson* don't belong in the same sentence."

"Maybe you don't know him as well as you think you do," she said. "Bill made me laugh and feel better than I've felt in a while. Since long before the accident." Cullen opened his mouth to speak, but she continued. "But even if I swallowed a 'stupid' pill and threw caution to the wind, I would never get involved with Bill…with any man…because you and I are still married."

Relief washed over Cullen's face. "Good."

His response angered and confused her. Why would he care, if he wanted a divorce? "That's all you have to say?"

"What more do you want?"

"An apology," she said. "You charged in here assuming the worst without considering that Bill is your friend and I'm your wife."

"I haven't been thinking straight. I've…been working a lot."

"What's new?" She didn't need to explain, but she didn't want him thinking the worst of her. "Just so you know. I have been good. Very good. Doing everything you and Dr. Marshall told me to do. Which is more than I can say for you."

Lines creased Cullen's forehead. "I have no idea what you're talking about."

"You told me you had shifts to make up, but you haven't been here at all. Heaven only knows where you've been spending your nights."

A devilish grin lit up his face. "You're the jealous one."

"Am not." Okay, maybe a little. But no way would she admit that to him. "I was…worried."

"Worried."

More than she wanted to admit. More than he would ever know. "Yes."

His eyes softened. He grinned sheepishly. "The way I was worried about you and Bill."

Busted. Darn it. She nodded once, feeling stupid and petty and pathetic.

His gaze met hers. "No need for you to worry. I stayed at a friend's place near the hospital so I could sleep more between shifts."

"Makes sense to stay with a friend."

But she didn't know if his "friend" was male or a buxom blonde named Bambi. And she wanted to know. Badly.

Cullen strode toward the couch. "I'm learning how important it is to have friends. I realize I've been taking them for granted."

The way he'd taken her for granted. But he'd never considered her a friend. Her throat tightened.

She should say something, but she hadn't a clue what. "You shouldn't get a pet if you're gone so much."

His eyes widened. "I don't always work this many shifts. A cat might work. As you said, they're independent."

"Even cats need to feel wanted and loved."

Not that he wanted and loved her, but once he had. At least, that was what he'd told her.

Cullen stood next to her.

Sarah's pulse skittered. Tension simmered between them. She shouldn't want him to kiss her. But she did. Badly.

Look away. Move away. But she couldn't—okay, didn't want to. Instead she was mesmerized by his blue eyes and full lips.

Once again she was reminded of magma rising. Only this time moving closer to the surface, where the gas pressure increased, accelerating faster and faster until erupting.

She wet her lips.

"In case you're still worried, the friend I stayed with—he's an anesthesiologist from the hospital," he said.

The surge of relief did nothing to douse the flame building inside her, threatening to explode. "Thanks."

The blue of his eyes deepened. "Thank you."

"For what?"

"This." Cullen lowered his mouth to hers and kissed her. Hard.

Heaven. His kiss made Sarah feel like she had died and gone to heaven. Best to enjoy every second, every minute if she was that lucky. She had a feeling this might be as close as she ever got to the pearly gates while her heart still beat. And beating it was.

In triple time.

His lips moved over hers with skill and familiarity. The kiss brought her home, back to where she'd longed to be for months now…in his arms. She'd thought about him, dreamed about him, missed him, even though she should have been getting over him. And now she realized why she was having so much trouble getting over him. He tasted warm and inviting. This was a yummy, comfy place she never wanted to leave. Each touch of his mouth, of his hands, made her tingle inside.

Forget pain medication—this was all she needed to feel better. Her blood simmered, rushing through her veins. It had been so long, too long, since she'd felt wanted. She didn't want the feeling to end.

His hand ran up her back, caressing her, until her hair was running through his fingers.

More. She wanted more.

Sarah parted her lips. He accepted the invitation and deepened the kiss, pressing harder against her mouth.

He'd followed her lead. It was time to follow his.

Her tongue reacquainted itself with him, exploring the recesses of his mouth. She remembered all the times they'd kissed before. Remembered the good times in their marriage when she had believed it would last forever. Maybe her memories were hazy because of the concussion, but this kiss felt different. Better, somehow.

She didn't want to analyze it too deeply. She wanted to...enjoy.

Heat pooled deep inside her. Need ached. Grew.

A moan escaped her lips.

More. Please.

Cullen drew her closer. She arched into him, only to come to an abrupt stop. She crashed into something hard, sending a jagged pain through her sore and healing abdomen. Her lips slipped off his. Spots appeared before her eyes.

Pain weakened her knees. It hurt, almost burned, so badly, but she didn't fall. Cullen held on to her.

He groaned, but didn't let go.

Sarah forced herself to breathe. A knife seemed to be slicing through her midsection. She straightened, intensifying the pain more. She looked down.

Stupid cast.

With the permanent bend in her elbow, her arm was stuck in position, a barrier between them.

In spite of her stomach hurting, she couldn't deny her reaction to Cullen's kisses. Her swollen and bruised lips throbbed. Her heart beat wildly. Her pulse hadn't settled.

She wanted to rewind time and relieve each second of his kisses.

Stupid. Dumb.

Forget about the cast getting in the way—she should have known better than to kiss him back the way she had. "I'm so sorry."

Cullen bent over, gasping for air. "Give me a sec."

The rasp in his voice made Sarah look at her cast. "More dangerous than I imagined."

He glanced up at her. "You have no idea."

Sarah reached toward him, then thought better of it. If she touched him, she would kiss him again. She pressed her left hand against her side. Pain made her want to sit. She leaned against the couch. "You okay?"

He straightened. "I can breathe now. How about you?"

Her senses reeled. Her heart screamed for more kisses. Her incisions hurt. "I've been better. But the pain's subsiding quicker than it usually does."

Cullen's mouth twisted. He looked so serious. As if the fate of the world rested on his shoulders and he'd screwed things up. "This was…"

"A mistake." Better for her to admit it before him. She should never have kissed him back. "If you're worried I'm thinking this changes things between us, don't be. The other kiss didn't. This one won't, either."

He didn't say a word, but his dark gaze remained on her.

"Kisses are an old habit for us. The opportunity arose again. I wanted to be kissed. It was bound to happen," she rambled, trying to justify what had occurred. "Someday we'll look back at this and laugh."

He raised a brow. "You think?"

She had no idea, but laughing this off was better than analyzing it to death and not liking her conclusion. "Sure."

"Most kisses aim for romance, not humor."

Was he aiming for romance by kissing her? Her pulse accelerated. No more kisses. "True, but romantic kisses are a dime a dozen. This one…"

A grin tugged at his lips. He rubbed his stomach. "I won't be forgetting this one anytime soon."

Her neither. But for different reasons than his.

Warning bells sounded in her head. Who was she kidding? She was past the warning stage. Alarms blared.

Best not to travel this road again. Giving in to desire would lead to disappointment and heartache. She couldn't do that to herself, to her heart. "But it won't happen again."

"Definitely not."

That was fast. Almost too fast. And he had said *probably* before, but *definitely* this time. Disappointment spiraled to the tips of her toes. At least they agreed, right?

She pressed her lips together, unsure what to say or do next. That seemed to be standard operating procedure whenever she was around Cullen. So why had she been so eager to see him when she woke up this morning?

He walked into the kitchen. "You mentioned taking a nap. While you sleep, I'll figure out dinner. I'm sure we have enough leftovers."

"It's Taco Night at the brewpub."

"You're in pain."

She didn't want to stay inside, with him so close and her aching with surprise need. "I want to go out."

His gaze raked over her, assessing her like one of his patients. "It'll be too much for you after such a long day."

"I've done nothing but lie or sit around, except for a walk outside with Bill."

Cullen's eyes narrowed. "There's snow on the ground. You could have slipped."

"We didn't go far, and Bill never let go of my arm."

"How gentlemanly of him."

Sarah didn't appreciate Cullen's sarcastic tone, but

maybe she could use this to her advantage. "Do you want to go to the brewpub tonight or not?"

"I like Taco Night, but I'm happy to stay home tonight. It's been a long week."

She empathized with that. "You must be exhausted."

He opened the refrigerator. "Let's go next week."

"You can go then." She straightened. "I'm going tonight. I'll call Bill."

Cullen slammed the fridge door. "Why do you want to go so badly?"

"I'm desperate to get out of the house."

He arched a brow. "Desperate?"

Sarah nodded. "I've been doing everything I'm supposed to do, but enough is enough. I need to get out and do something. Have…"

"Fun," he finished for her.

It would be fun to kiss him again. She didn't dare admit that. "Lying around all day resting is the antithesis of fun. I can sit at the brewpub as easily as I can here."

"You won't be here alone."

That was the problem tonight. She was alone with him. "I've enjoyed having people around. Everyone is nice and we're getting to know each other. But I need to get out, have a change of environment, scenery, whatever you want to call it, or I'm going to lose my mind."

Or burn with unspent desire.

Kissing Cullen again would send her over the edge completely.

Going to the brewpub made the most sense. The other option—spending the evening at home with Cullen—didn't seem like a smart idea. Sure, they'd agreed not to kiss again, but they'd also agreed to divorce. Who knew what could happen with the two of them here alone tonight? She didn't want to take any chances. She couldn't afford more kisses. She couldn't lose her heart to him. That would destroy her.

"Leanne told me about the soft pretzels with the house dipping sauce," Sarah explained. "I love pretzels."

"I didn't know that."

She wished he had made more time for her so they could have gotten to know each other better.

"I didn't know about your broken arm." Sarah waited for him to respond. She didn't understand his hesitation. "If you'd rather stay home, that's fine. Bill will drive me if you're not up for it."

Cullen's nostrils flared. "I'm up for it."

"But you said—"

"I changed my mind, okay?"

More than okay. She didn't care if jealousy was the reason or not, even if it gave her an unexpected rush of feminine power. "It's great. Thanks."

"Take a short nap first," he ordered in that oh-so-strict doctor's voice of his.

Such a change from the way he'd been kissing and touching her a few minutes ago. She gave a mock salute. "Aye, aye, Captain. Pillows are fluffed and the sheet turned down ready for nap, sir."

If only he'd join her...

Playful images flitted through her mind. Her temperature rose.

On second thought, napping by herself was better. Safer. Even if she would be...lonelier.

CHAPTER NINE

TACO NIGHT AT the Hood Hamlet Brewpub always put a smile on Cullen's face. Nothing beat good food, great beer and hanging with friends, but it was the last place he wanted to be tonight. He gripped the steering wheel and turned onto Main Street, trying to ignore the floral scent of Sarah's shampoo drifting his way.

She peered out the window. "It's crowded for a Thursday."

Her kisses had sent him to the brink. He'd been on the verge of losing all control until she'd taken him out with her cast. He'd never been so relieved to be punched in the gut. It hurt, but he could have been hurt a lot more if he'd continued kissing her. "Fresh snowfall brings skiers and riders to the mountain."

Sarah turned toward him. "What about climbers?"

His gaze lingered on her lips. He jerked his attention back to the road. She was the one with the concussion, but he needed to have his head examined. Imagining her with Paulson during the drive home had done crazy things to Cullen.

His self-control had been nonexistent. Whenever Sarah was involved, his feelings overrode common sense. But he hadn't withdrawn or run away from her. This time he'd done something worse. He'd kissed her.

Talk about reckless behavior.

Finding out *she* was jealous about who he was with had been a real turn-on. Kissing her had seemed the most natural thing in the world. But he couldn't allow himself to be taken in by her again. "If they're smart, they'll wait for a better weather window and an avalanche report."

"If not?"

"You hope they get lucky. Otherwise OMSAR pings us with a mission call out."

"Some people think they can conquer the mountain."

He parked across the street from the brewpub. "Yeah, but the mountain always wins."

"Mother Nature gets a shot in once in a while."

"Leanne's fiancé, Christian, can tell you all about that."

"She mentioned how OMSAR rescued his cousin and him."

Cullen turned off the ignition. "They got caught in a wicked storm, but it ended well."

Sarah unfastened her seat belt. "It's too bad there aren't more happy endings like that."

Her wistful tone surprised him. Sarah could be impulsive, but she didn't give in to flights of fancy or fairy tales. She must be talking about her rescue. "Yours has a happy ending."

Her gaze narrowed. "What are you talking about?"

"Mount Baker. Your accident," he explained. "Your data could have been destroyed. Your injuries could have been worse. You could have died. But none of those things happened. Happy ending."

"It will be happy once I'm back at the institute."

Away from him.

The words were unspoken, but implied. They stung, given how passionately she'd kissed him back this afternoon.

She reached across her chest and fumbled with the door handle.

He leaned over to help. His arm brushed her breast, sending a burst of heat rushing through him. He pulled back. "Sorry."

"I've got it." On the third try she opened the door.

She exited as if a bomb were about to blow. He hurried around the truck, then held her hand. "Be careful."

Annoyance burned in the depths of Sarah's eyes. She tugged her hand out of his. "I know to be careful."

"Just watching out for you."

"It's not as if I did something stupid to make myself fall. If the steam blast hadn't happened…"

She wouldn't be here. The thought brought a strange mix of relief and regret.

"I can cross the street by myself," she continued.

"There could be ice," he cautioned. She must be hungry. Hunger would explain her short fuse. "I'd say the same thing to anyone else who was with me, so don't get your panties in a twist."

She pursed her lips. "That would be hard to do, since I'm not wearing panties."

Cullen's mouth went dry. His gaze dropped to her hips. All he saw were jeans, but the thoughts running through his head raised his temperature twenty degrees.

"Trust me, I'd know if my thong was twisted," she added.

A thong. He remembered her thongs. His temperature spiraled. He needed to take off his jacket.

He realized a moment too late she was crossing the street without him. "Wait up, Lavagirl."

Sarah stood on the sidewalk, tapping her toe.

"You're hungry," he said.

Her foot stopped moving. She nodded with a contrite expression.

"The taco bar is all-you-can-eat," he said.

She bit her lip.

He motioned her toward the entrance, but she didn't move.

Her gaze filled with uncertainty. "Is there anything I should know before we go inside?"

"About the taco bar?"

"About the people I'm going to meet."

Not only hungry. Nervous. "You've met Carly, Zoe, Hannah and Leanne."

"And Bill."

Unfortunately. Cullen wasn't too happy with Paulsen right now. "Jake Porter, Sean Hughes and Christian Welton, if he's not on duty, will be here. I'm not sure about Hannah and Garrett Willingham or Rita and Tim Moreno, since they need babysitters. You never know who will show up. But no worries. Everybody will make you feel right at home."

An older couple holding hands exited the brewpub. Sarah stepped aside to let them pass. Cullen did the same.

Sarah glanced at the door to the brewpub as if it were a black hole. "I'll make sure I don't embarrass you in front of your friends."

"You've never embarrassed me."

"That time I danced on the bar at the hole-in-the-wall dive near Joshua Tree."

The taste of tequila shots with lemon and salt

rushed back. He remembered the way she'd moved to the pulse-pounding music. "I was turned on, not embarrassed. I would have preferred a private performance without the other men leering at you. Then you could have taken it all off and not just undone only a couple of buttons."

"Well, then—" she flipped her hair behind her shoulder in a seamless, sexy move that nearly cut him to his knees "—I guess I have nothing to worry about tonight."

She might not, but Cullen couldn't say the same thing. He had a feeling he would be worrying for as long as Sarah was in town. Maybe even after she left.

Being out should have perked up Sarah's spirits and energized her like a toy bunny with brand-new batteries. But as soon as she stepped inside the brew-pub, the smells of hops and grease assaulted her. Her stomach churned, not with hunger, but a severe case of nerves.

Rock music played, but the din of conversation drowned out the lyrics. Servers dressed in jeans and black T-shirts carried pitchers of beers, pint glasses and sodas.

"They're in the back," Cullen said.

She had no idea how he'd found his friends among all the people, but she followed him, weaving around crowded tables and past jam-packed booths. She ignored the strong impulse to grab his hand.

That would be a bad move. Just like kissing him back and coming here. Sarah should have stayed at the cabin, locked away in her bedroom, where she wouldn't be so hypersensitive. She didn't know if it was aftereffects of his kiss or the anticipation of meeting more of his friends or...

Yours is a happy ending.

Yeah, that was what had gotten her panties—make that thong—in a twist and turned her insides into a quivering mess.

Sarah wanted a happily-ever-after of her own. Once upon a time she thought she'd found hers with Cullen. But she should have known it wasn't meant to be. As a child, she might have dreamed of living a storybook-type life, but she'd learned the chances of happily ever after were slim to none. She accepted that reality, though she hated it.

You were no longer a part of my life. I could start over in Hood Hamlet with a clean slate once the divorce was finalized.

She'd thought the same thing about living without him before her accident. Now she wasn't so sure.

Cullen had found the perfect place to spend the rest of his life, to fall in love, get married again and raise a family. She would return to the institute, work until her grant was over then find another job at a volcano somewhere else in the world. That adventurous way of life had always appealed to her.

Until now.

What was she thinking? She loved what she did. Work fulfilled her. It was her life.

The confusion, envy and dissatisfaction had to be from the concussion and her injuries, tiredness and hunger. Once she ate, she would feel better.

Cullen motioned to a long table with attractive men sitting on one end and beautiful women on the other. "Looks like most of the crew made it."

Bill sat with two men Sarah hadn't seen before. Cullen fit right in with that bunch of eye candy.

Zoe Hughes waved. She wore a colorful sleeveless shirt with ruffles on the front. A sparkly clip held up her hair with stylish, artfully placed tendrils around her face. "Leanne said we might see you tonight. I'm so glad you came."

Sarah wasn't used to people being so happy to see her. It felt good. "It took some convincing, but the good doctor finally relented."

Cullen raised his hands. "I know when to surrender."

Zoe's blue eyes twinkled. "Proud of you, Doc."

Introductions were made and a pitcher of Jake's handcrafted root beer ordered for Sarah.

Leanne shooed him away. "Go sit with the guys, Doc, so us girls can chat."

Cullen pulled a chair out for Sarah. "Let me know when you're ready to eat. I'll go with you to the taco bar. It'll be hard for you with one hand."

With a nod, she sat.

He pushed in her chair, then joined his friends a few feet away.

Carly pushed her long blond hair behind her ears. "Cullen is so overprotective of you."

Leanne nodded. "I always knew there was more to him than met the eye."

"It's so sweet." Zoe sighed. "I can't imagine what Sean would be like if I was injured in an accident. I doubt he'd let me out of his sight or want me to do anything, either."

As if Cullen loved Sarah that much. A lead weight settled in the bottom of her stomach. He might care, he might be concerned, but not the way a devoted husband would be if something happened to his beloved wife.

Sarah glanced his way.

Tenderness filled his gaze.

Her heart bumped. Flustered, she looked away.

"You have more color than this morning," Leanne said. "Feeling better?"

Sarah might still be flushed after being kissed

so thoroughly. Or it could be embarrassment. She cleared her throat. "I went for a walk today with Bill. Got some fresh air."

"And now the brewpub," Carly said. "That's more excitement than you're used to."

Especially when you added in Cullen's kisses. Sarah nodded.

The server placed a pitcher of root beer and a glass on the table. Cullen already had a beer in his hand. Carly filled the glass and gave it to Sarah.

"Thanks." She took a sip. Thick and rich with the right amount of sweetness. "This is great."

Carly grinned. "Jake makes the best root beer in Oregon."

Leanne grinned. "The two of you are so cute. You act like newlyweds, even with a baby."

"Nicki is officially a toddler now," Carly said.

Sarah noticed how Jake and Carly smiled at each other a lot. The same with Sean and Zoe.

A diamond-engagement-ring-size lump lodged in Sarah's throat. These happy couples gave her hope some marriages could succeed. They also were a harsh reminder of how hers had failed.

How did some people get so lucky? That was what she wanted to know.

A plate with two large pretzels and a small bowl of mustard dipping sauce appeared in front of her.

She looked over her shoulder to see Cullen standing there.

He smiled. "You wanted to try a pretzel."

His gesture touched her. If only they could have been one of the lucky couples. "I do."

"The pretzels are almost as good as the root beer," Carly said.

Zoe flipped her hair. "The pretzels are better."

"Try one," Cullen urged.

"Listen to the good doctor," Leanne said. "He would never lead you astray."

No, he had only turned Sarah's world inside out by making her believe happy endings were possible. But they weren't for her. She took another sip of her root beer.

Cullen held a piece of pretzel in front of her face. Mustard covered an end. "Open up."

The lump in her throat doubled. She looked up at him.

A devilish smile curved his lips. "You know you want it."

Her heart slammed against her chest. What was he doing? This felt like…flirting.

As he brought the pretzel closer, wicked laughter lit his eyes.

She parted her lips and cautiously bit off the end of the pretzel. The bread, salt and mustard sauce complemented each other perfectly. But she was more interested in the way Cullen looked at her—as though he wanted to taste her.

"How is the pretzel?" Jake asked.

The pretzel. Right. She focused on the men at the far end of the table. "Delicious. Like the root beer."

But not quite as yummy as Cullen. Her pulse picked up speed, accelerating as if she were tumbling downhill. Which was what she'd be doing if she didn't stop acting like a lovesick teenager. She looked away to find Zoe, Leanne and Carly staring at her with rapt interest.

Sarah sipped her root beer. She understood their curiosity. Cullen feeding her made them seem like a couple. She had no idea what was going on and wasn't sure she had the strength to find out. Kissing him had been bad enough. Getting her hopes up and then discovering this was another fantasy would hurt worse than being hit by another steam blast.

No, thank you.

On the drive home from the brewpub, Sarah closed her eyes. The evening had taken its toll, physically as well as emotionally. If anything, seeing Carly and Jake Porter and Zoe and Sean Hughes together had made Sarah realize how far apart she and Cullen really were. And always had been. She sighed, not a sigh of frustration but of resignation for what would never be.

The truck's engine stopped. She opened her eyes. The porch light illuminated the path to the cabin's front door through the darkness. The night was playing tricks on her vision. The distance appeared longer than it really was. Too bad that wasn't the case with the separation between her and Cullen and their dreams.

"Tired?" Cullen sounded concerned.

Through the shadows in the truck's cab, she saw his worried gaze upon her. Their situation would be easier to handle if he didn't act as though he cared what happened to her.

Cullen is so overprotective of you.

Too bad he was the same way with everyone he knew. Strangers, too. "I'm a little tired."

That gave her a good excuse to go straight to her room. No reason to linger and wish for what might have been or a good-night kiss.

Not. Going. To. Happen.

Sarah climbed out of the truck and hurried to the front door.

Cullen followed at her heels. "Slow down."

Sarah didn't. She couldn't. All the happy couples tonight were an in-her-face reminder. She wasn't like the women she'd been with tonight. She would never have the perfect kind of wedded and domestic bliss the others had achieved. She could never be a perfect, proper wife. She wasn't made that way.

He unlocked and opened the door.

Sarah stepped inside ready to retreat to her room, but a hand touched her left shoulder. She nearly jumped.

"Let's sit for a minute," Cullen said, so close she could smell him, musky and warm and inviting.

The ache in her stomach increased. "Can't this wait until morning?"

"No." He led her to the sofa. "It won't take long."

Of course it wouldn't. Cullen never liked to talk. Sarah remembered all the times she'd needed to talk to him, but he'd retreated and left her more upset. She didn't want to do the same thing to him. She took a seat.

He sat next to her. "You looked like you were having fun tonight."

She nodded. "Your friends are very nice."

"They like you," he said. "Especially Paulson."

Sarah blew out a breath. "Bill's harmless."

"As harmless as a howitzer tank and about as subtle."

That made her smile.

"I'm glad you talked me into going," Cullen said. "Seeing you with everyone tonight. Laughing and joking. It's like you've been a part of the group for-ever."

Sarah stiffened. "What do you mean? I'm nothing like your friends. They're so…domestic."

"Paulson isn't."

"*Domestic* isn't the right word." She backtracked. "What I mean is they're caretakers. They look out for each other. All for one. I'm more of an…adventurer."

"Your research will save lives in the future. I don't know how much more of a caretaker you could be."

Cullen was wrong. She could never be the kind of wife he wanted. "I'm a loner, not the family type. Nothing like Carly, Zoe and Hannah. Or your mother and sisters…"

"What about my mom and sisters?" he asked.

Oops. Sarah hadn't meant to say that aloud. "It's nothing."

"Let me be the judge of that."

"It's just…" Sarah rubbed her mouth. "Well, it was pretty obvious your family didn't like me much."

Cullen flinched as if she'd slapped him. "That's not true."

Sarah raised her left shoulder, but she knew her gut instincts were 100 percent correct. She wasn't proper wife material. "It is. The way your family acted that Easter. I've never felt so inadequate in my life."

He made a face. "Come on."

The disbelief in his voice set her nerves even more on edge. She hadn't fitted into his family's out-of-this world holiday at all. "I wanted to help with dinner. I tried to help. But I only got in their way. They kicked me out of the kitchen and told me to go find you."

"That's because they didn't want to put you to work. You were a guest."

"A guest." The word tasted like ash in her mouth. "I was your wife. I thought I was family."

She'd wanted to be family. More than anything. But that hadn't happened. She could never be the kind of wife he would want. That was when she'd realized his family would never accept her and Cullen wouldn't want her.

Tears welled in her eyes. She blinked them away.

He started to speak, then stopped himself.

Sarah wasn't surprised he had nothing more to say. She picked at the cast's padding around her fingers.

Cullen leaned toward her. "I should have told you. Warned you."

The regret, thick and heavy, in his voice shocked her. "About what?"

His clouded gaze met hers. "Easter. My family. Blaine."

"What does your twin brother have to do with this?" she asked.

"Everything."

The one word sent a chill down Sarah's spine. Cullen's grief and sadness were as clear as they'd been that afternoon at Red Rocks when he'd mentioned his twin brother who had died. That was the one and only time he'd spoken of Blaine. She'd asked a few questions, but he'd never answered them.

She reached for his hand. His skin felt cold, not warm as usual. "You told me Blaine died when you were in college."

"He died on Easter."

Surprise washed over her. Cullen had never told her any details. "On Easter Sunday?"

Cullen nodded. His hand wrapped around hers. Squeezed. "Blaine used to love Easter. He always wanted more decorations and food. There were never enough eggs and candy for him. Because of what happened, my family goes all out on the holiday. Overcompensates."

She sat back, stunned and angry he hadn't shared this information with her. Not telling her about breaking his arm as a kid was one thing, but this...

Easter weekend with the Grays had been the tipping point for her to bring up divorce. She'd realized then it was only a matter of time before Cullen checked out of their marriage for good.

"I..." A million thoughts swirled through her

mind, but she didn't know where to begin. "I had no idea."

Cullen scooted closer. His thigh pressed against hers. Self-preservation urged her to move away from him, but she hated that he was hurting.

His gaze locked on hers. "It's not just Easter. Putting on over-the-top holidays and birthdays, especially mine, is my family's way of dealing with grief and the empty place at the table."

Easter hadn't been as perfect as she'd imagined—far from it actually. The realization left her off-kilter. With this new information she tried to relate how she'd felt then.

His family sure had put on a good act. She'd never sensed what was going on beneath the surface. She'd been so focused on her own insecurities she hadn't thought what the holidays would mean to them after losing a son and a brother. But she wasn't about to give Cullen a free pass over this. "You should have talked to me about this. You realize I don't even know how Blaine died?"

"My brother was a drug addict." Cullen's voice cracked, but his gaze never wavered from hers. "Blaine died of an overdose. I like to think it was accidental, but who knows? I found him unconscious when I went to get him for Easter dinner."

Horror flooded her. She gripped his hand, ignoring the urge to hold him. "Oh, Cullen. I'm so sorry."

"Me, too." Self-recriminations twisted his lips. "I failed Blaine. Interventions. Rehab. Tough love. I tried everything I could and I still couldn't save him."

Her heart ached for him, for all the Grays. "Addiction doesn't work that way."

"I know, but when it's your twin brother..."

"It's a horrible, impossible situation." Even knowing that, she couldn't begin to comprehend what Cullen had gone through, both when his brother was alive and afterward. Still, she wondered what else she might have misunderstood about him and his life. "If I'd known..."

It might have made a difference in their marriage. She could have understood why his family acted the way they had. She could have helped Cullen.

"I didn't want to burden you." He stroked her hand with his thumb. "I hadn't thought about how not knowing might affect you. I should have discussed this with you so you would understand."

"That would have helped. But I'm glad you told me now." Sarah waited for him to pull his hand away from hers. He didn't. Until he did, she would hold tight. She didn't want to break the connection with him. This was the most open Cullen had been with her, and she feared he would shut down or run away from her again. She didn't want that to happen. "I'm sorry for not asking about Blaine before and not trying to understand your family's behavior."

"We both kept secrets from each other."

Sarah nodded. She hadn't told him about her ex-fiancé.

Cullen had hidden his pain the same way she'd hidden hers. She'd protected herself and her heart, never trusting he'd stay in the relationship to fully open up to him. No doubt he'd felt the same way about her by not telling her about Blaine. Regrets grew exponentially until she struggled to breathe.

"We're quite the pair." Distrusting and afraid to let anyone in. Their marriage had never stood a chance without that kind of openness—the kind of openness that would have allowed him to tell her the truth about his brother and family. The kind of openness that wouldn't have blinded her to Cullen's and his family's grief. "Holding back didn't help our marriage."

"No, but it feels good to let it all out finally."

Seeing him like this reminded her of when they'd first met. He'd had no problem talking to her in Red Rocks. She'd always wondered how he could have been so open there, but not when they returned to Seattle.

"Anything else you want to tell me?" Sarah tried to sound lighthearted. She wasn't sure she succeeded.

"There's nothing left to tell." His gaze raked over her. "Besides, you're tired."

Her chest tightened. She was losing him. He was retreating behind the doctor persona. But she wanted dearly to hang on to the moment. "I'm okay."

He pulled his hand away.

A deep ache welled within her soul. She missed his warmth. She missed…him.

"Your eyelids look heavy," he said in that professional tone of his she was beginning to hate. "It's past time for your medicine."

Despite herself, she stifled a yawn. Now that he mentioned it, her long day *was* catching up to her. But she hated to let things end this way. "I can stay up a little while longer. I'm feeling okay."

His eyes softened, not quite the look a physician gave a patient, but not one a loving husband gave to his wife. Soon to be ex-wife. "The goal is to have you feeling better than okay."

Once she was better, she could return to Bellingham—except right now going back didn't appeal to her as much as it once had. Not when she wanted to recapture the closeness they'd just shared.

Every nerve ending screeched.

What was she thinking? Bellingham was where

she belonged. She couldn't allow this moment—this *one* conversation—to change anything. That would be stupid.

Risking her heart again because he'd opened up for a glimmer of what could have been would only hurt her in the end. Sarah had to stay focused on what was best for her. That was getting back to work—the one thing that wouldn't let her down.

She stood. "You're right. I'm more tired than I realized. I'm going to bed."

In the kitchen, Cullen washed his hands, then filled a glass with water. He stretched his neck to each side, but couldn't quite unknot all his tight muscles.

His talk with Sarah hadn't gone as he'd expected. He'd wanted to know what she thought of his friends and the brewpub. He'd never planned on talking about Blaine. No one outside his family and close friends back home knew the truth, but Cullen had been compelled to tell her. He needed to rectify the mistake he'd made by not saying anything about Blaine before. She'd needed to understand that what had happened at Easter wasn't her fault.

He tore a paper towel off the roll, then dispensed her medications.

I've never felt so inadequate in my life.

The pain in those eight words, the tears gleaming

in her eyes, had been like daggers to his heart. Cullen hadn't wanted her to cry. She'd been hurt enough.

Because of him.

He'd wanted only to appease his family, particularly his mother, after missing the Easter before. Thanksgiving and Christmas, too. He hadn't considered Sarah's feelings during that trip home. He hadn't considered her much at all when they were together.

Expressing too much emotion equaled loss of self-control, especially around Sarah, who had a way of tearing down his walls. But his silence—not talking and warning her how hard Easter was for his family—had set her up for failure.

He couldn't undo the past, but he wanted to make it up to her somehow. Sarah had difficulty using her laptop and working for more than a few minutes. An idea formed…a way to help her do her job from the cabin. He could take care of that tomorrow.

Cullen walked to her bedroom. He knocked on the closed door, careful not to spill any water. He didn't want Sarah to slip the next time she exited her room.

No answer.

He tried again.

Nothing.

A frisson of worry shot to the surface. He opened the door. "Sarah?"

She was lying on her back in the center of the queen-size bed, sound asleep. Her dark hair was spread across the pillowcase. She'd taken off her jacket and removed her boots, but she was still wearing her jeans and red henley shirt.

I'm a little tired.

A little? Try a lot. Their discussion in the living room hadn't helped matters.

"Sarah." Cullen placed the water glass and medicine on the nightstand. He gently touched her left arm. "Wake up. You need to take your medicine."

Her heavy eyelids cracked. "Must I?"

"You must."

With some effort, she sat. "I thought you were a good doctor."

"I'm a very good doctor, which is why you have to do this."

"I was sleeping fine without them."

"We want you to wake up feeling fine in the morning."

She blinked. "*We?* There hasn't been a *we* for a while."

"That's true." Cullen regretted contributing so much to that happening. "But we're here together now, and we both want you to recover."

Sarah nodded once. She took the pills from him and put them into her mouth.

He handed her the water.

She sipped and swallowed. "Thanks. Now I'm going back to sleep."

"After you undress."

Sarah rested her head against the pillow and closed her eyes. "I'm too tired."

Sleeping in her clothes would be uncomfortable, but she was an adult. Controlling Sarah never was something he'd wanted to do. Or could do for that matter. He wanted only to control her influence on him. "At least get out of your jeans."

Her eyelids fluttered. "I'm not sure I can. I still have trouble with the button when I'm wide-awake."

"Want help?" he offered.

"Please. If you wouldn't mind."

Mind? He wasn't sure what he felt at the moment, but this seemed a light penance for his wrongdoings with her.

His fingers trembled with anticipation and need. He touched the button on her waistband.

Get a grip, Gray.

This had nothing to do with sex. He was supposed to help her. He wanted to help her, if only to make amends for what he'd put her through. But the crazy push-pull of regret versus the physical attraction was giving him whiplash.

Cullen unbuttoned the waistband of her jeans. He

tugged down on the zipper. The teeth of the zipper released. This wasn't so hard. He glimpsed a patch of pink lace.

His groin tightened. He jerked his hand away.

They might be soon-to-be divorced and she might be the last woman in the world he should want to be with, but that did nothing to lessen his attraction. His reaction had nothing to do with being celibate for nearly a year. It was Sarah. No one else had ever made him feel like this.

He liked that. Liked how she'd held his hand tonight as he talked about Blaine. Liked how she trusted him to help her in spite of all his failures.

"It's okay. I've got it," she mumbled.

Suck it up, Gray. Any fool could see she was exhausted. He needed to think about her, not himself. "Go back to sleep. I'll take care of it."

That was the least he could do.

Cullen pulled her jeans over the curve of her hips and down her thighs. His hand touched her skin. He ignored the sparks arcing through his fingertips with each brush and slid the jeans all the way off.

Sarah lay on the bed. Her eyes closed. Her lips parted.

Cullen wondered what she dreamed about. Him? If only…

He wanted to crawl into bed next to her and hold

her, not only until the sun came up, but…forever. He yearned for the future he'd dreamed of having with her. But that wasn't what she wanted. Even if she did, it might not be the best thing for her. He didn't know how to act or how to be more open. But maybe with Sarah's help, he could learn.…

CHAPTER TEN

SUNLIGHT WARMED SARAH'S face. She opened her eyes. Light flooded the room through the open blinds. Usually she closed them before she went to bed.

But last night hadn't been usual. Cullen had opened up to her in a way she'd never expected. He'd given her medicine and removed her jeans. But no goodnight kiss or even a peck on the forehead.

Sarah had been…disappointed. She chalked up the reaction to exhaustion. The last things she needed were any more kisses.

She shrugged on her robe, tied the strap as best as she could and walked out of her room. She had no idea whether Hannah, Leanne or Zoe would be here this morning. Sarah had a feeling Bill wouldn't be back.

She entered the living room.

"Good morning," Bill said, holding on to a ream of paper.

She did a double take. "You're babysitting me today?"

"Nope, I am." Cullen sat on the floor next to a leather recliner working on a printer.

Sarah looked around the living room filled with cords and boxes, the chair and a table she'd never seen before. "What's going on?"

Bill grinned as if he'd eaten three canaries and two parrots. "You know how your head hurts and arm aches when you work on your laptop?"

She knew the feelings all too well. "Yes."

"Well, we had a great idea—"

"We?" Cullen asked.

The firefighter winked. "Doc had the idea to set up a more comfortable workstation for you."

"You can print pages if the screen gives you a headache," Cullen said.

She covered her mouth with her hands. "This is…"

His gaze met hers. "Not exactly the definition of *fun*."

"It's mine." She studied the oversize leather recliner. "Where did the chair come from?"

He motioned his head toward Bill. "Paulson is good for a few things."

"A lot of things, if you happen to be a lovely lady." Bill ran his fingertips along the buttery leather. "This is my favorite chair. It's yours for as long as you need it."

"Thank you," Sarah said. "Thanks to both of you. But you shouldn't have gone to so much trouble."

Cullen stood. "You need more to do than sleep and walk. Some data analysis won't hurt you if you don't overdo it."

Sarah couldn't believe he'd listened to what she'd said yesterday when they'd spoken about going to Taco Night and done something about it. Something so wonderful.

Her heart swelled with joy. Maybe Cullen had changed. Heaven knew he kept surprising her with each passing day. "I can't wait to get to work."

He brushed his hands together. "Breakfast first."

"What are we having?" Bill asked.

"Omelets and bacon, but I need to run to the store for more eggs."

"I'll go," Bill said, then took off.

She wanted to kiss Cullen and not only with kisses of gratitude. Her heart lodged itself in her throat. "Thank you."

"Your work's important. This will make things easier on you."

And be the perfect distraction. She needed something to keep her from throwing herself into his arms and smothering his gorgeous face with kisses. "Are you working tonight?"

"Nope. I'm caught up on the shifts I missed," he

said. "I got lucky. I only missed four shifts while I was away."

She looked at Bill's chair and the table with the printer. Cullen had set up everything on the left-hand side. A rush of affection infused her. "I feel lucky myself."

Last night everything in her world had seemed wrong. Today it felt oh-so-right. Sarah couldn't believe he'd gone to so much trouble. Her heart stumbled.

"It can't be easy having me here, but I appreciate everything you're doing and have done." She couldn't change what had happened in the past, but she was speaking from the heart now. Cullen was her Prince Charming, and she felt like a princess. Albeit a bruised and battered one, but a princess nonetheless. And this might be the closest she ever got to a happy ending. "I hope you know that."

His satisfied smile settled on his lips and spread to his twinkling blue eyes. "I do now."

Over the next week, Sarah slept less and worked more. Interpreting data gave her a sense of purpose and kept her from thinking about Cullen. Okay, thinking about him *too much*. She still dreamed about him and occasionally thought about him kissing her. Thankfully he didn't again.

No matter how compelling the fairy tale was, Sarah knew better than to buy into it again. Others shared true love's kiss and found a happily-ever-after. Not her. She needed to stay focused.

But being with Cullen made it easy to forget her goal wasn't to settle into a comfortable routine here. There might be room for her at the cabin, but there wasn't room in his life. A few conversations didn't make up for all the times he hadn't wanted to talk to her. His kind gestures touched her, but they didn't change anything. She needed to get back to Mount Baker, back to the institute, back to *her* life.

And that was what she intended to do.

Today was her first day alone, a big step on her road to a full recovery. She was enjoying her first taste of independence since the accident. Oh, she'd missed the smell of coffee when she woke and conversations with her friends. But this was what she needed in order to return to Bellingham.

After eating lunch, Sarah downloaded files from MBVI's server. She studied a data stream her boss wanted her to check. The seismometer appeared to be working properly. She'd looked at enough of these squiggly lines to know the difference between ice movement and data glitches, but something didn't make sense. Magma shouldn't move without generating more specific seismic signals. At least, she'd never seen that before.

Sarah opened a new tab on her browser and checked a website listing the many earthquakes that occurred daily in the Pacific Northwest. She scratched her head. "What am I missing here?"

"Me?"

A bevy of butterflies took flight, turning her stomach into a crowded butterfly house. She had missed him, even if she shouldn't.

As he walked toward her, his aquamarine polo shirt seemed to change the shade of his blue eyes, reminding her of Los Tenideros in Costa Rica's Tenorio Volcano National Park, where two different-colored rivers merge. She'd traveled there after receiving her PhD and before starting at MBVI. She'd hoped the trip would heal the wound from her aborted marriage. Hadn't worked. She now wondered if anything could do that.

Sarah couldn't believe how good it was to see Cullen. A part of her wanted to fling herself into his arms, which would be a really stupid thing to do. She remained seated.

He smiled, a wide smile showing off straight white teeth and crinkling the corners of his eyes. He looked gorgeous. Even more so than usual.

She gripped her laptop. "I didn't hear you come in."

"That's what happens when you're concentrating."

His tone teased, but he was right. She'd lost herself in her work and forgotten about everything else. She could lose herself in Cullen if she wasn't careful. "I may be trying too hard."

He stood next to her, looking over her shoulder. "Head hurt?"

His concern warmed her like a fleece blanket. All she'd wanted was to be special to him. But he cared about everyone's well-being, not just hers. That was one reason he'd become a doctor. He'd mentioned Blaine as the other. She hadn't understood why until last week. Cullen might not have been able to save his twin brother, but he was doing his best to save others. "My head is fine. The data is causing me problems."

"Wrong?"

"Data is data. It can't be wrong. But my interpretation might be off," she admitted. "Things are inconclusive right now. I have a suspicion I may have started with too many preconceived notions."

He leaned forward, putting his hand on her shoulder. His male scent wrapped around her. His heat enveloped her. "Why do you think that?"

Cullen sounded interested, as if he really wanted to know what she was thinking. Tenderness and affection and attraction exploded in her chest. She glanced at the graph, trying to ignore her racing pulse, the pooling of desire, the longing for connection squeezing her tight. "Well…"

The numbers and lines blurred. She blinked. Everything was still fuzzy. Her head didn't hurt. It wasn't her concussion. All she could think about, all she wanted to see was…

Cullen.

Her heart pounded as hard as the surf ramming against the coast of Hawaii's Big Island.

Oh, no. She was falling for him.

Realization nearly bowled her over. Not quite the same explosive force of five hundred atomic bombs detonating as had marked the Mount Saint Helens eruption, but enough to send a chunk of molten lava crashing to the bottom of her stomach and taking up permanent residence there.

Sarah struggled to breathe. Whatever happened, she couldn't fall all the way. That would be catastrophic.

"Sarah?"

"I—I thought my gut instinct was correct." She forced words past the constriction in her throat. "I've been looking at data to support a hypothesis. Not looking at the data with an open mind."

Similar to what she'd done falling for him.

He sat on the couch. "It's not too late to go back over it."

"I'm sure I can remedy this."

Because she knew exactly where she'd gone wrong. Tucker wanted her back at the institute ASAP. He'd mentioned it again during their phone call this morning. She should have left by now. But she had stayed trying to work the data so she wouldn't have to go back.

Talk about stupid. She could be the poster child for the movement.

"Sarah?"

"Sorry." If she weren't careful he'd think she'd suffered another head injury. "I'm...frustrated."

She had a job to do. A responsibility to the institute. She'd messed up her analysis. Not to mention allowing her feelings for Cullen to...deepen.

"Hey, don't look so sad. It'll be okay." He touched her hand. "Cut yourself some slack. You're still recovering." He rubbed her hand. His calloused thumb made circles on her skin, leaving a trail of heat and tingles. "You've been working too hard."

Not hard enough. Sarah had become too distracted. She'd disregarded known facts and allowed herself to be caught up in a fantasy. Time to stop with the daydreams and focus on reality.

Cullen might not act the same as he had a year

ago, but she hadn't changed. Even if he was willing to give marriage another shot, the outcome would be the same. He would abandon her like everyone else in her life.

Sarah had to be strong. She squared her shoulders. "What are you doing home? I thought you would be at Timberline Lodge all day."

Amusement twinkled in his eyes. "Look out the window."

Big, fluffy snowflakes fell from the sky. "When did it start snowing?"

"A couple of hours ago," he said. "Hughes, Paulson and Moreno are out there now."

"Go join them." And let her try to save face, do her job correctly and get him out of her head and heart again.

Cullen continued to rub her hand. "I can do that another day. I wanted to see how you were doing."

A warm and fuzzy feeling trickled through her. *Pathetic.*

Sarah should be immune to him, not reacting like a lovesick teen to every word he said. She tilted her chin. "I'm doing well."

"Well, but frustrated."

He was part of her frustration. That gave her an idea. "You've been working hard. You need a break."

"You're the one who needs a break. Time away from the data so you can relax."

Time away from Cullen to clear her head. That might do the trick. She closed her laptop. "Sounds good. I'll take a nap. Grab your board and join your friends."

"I have a better idea. Let's take a break together."

Her heart rate resembled the data she'd been looking at. Inconsistent and all over the place. "Don't waste your free time on me."

"I'd rather enjoy it with you."

Sarah melted. She couldn't help it. She should decline politely. But the words wouldn't come. Not when her heart was clamoring so loudly it drowned out all sense of self-preservation.

Mischief, as worrisome as a ticking bomb, glinted in his eyes. "I know what we can do. Are you up to checking out Main Street with me?"

Temptation exploded with enough force to do significant damage. Sarah wanted to spend time with him. Be with him. She might regret this. Who was she kidding? She *would* regret this. But she didn't care. "I'm up for it."

As long as Cullen would be with her, she was up for anything.

Half an hour later, Cullen strolled down Main Street with Sarah at his side. She spun to see all the shops and sights. Her excitement added a bounce to his step.

A layer of snow clung to her black parka and colorful wool beanie. The cold air turned her cheeks a cute pink. She looked pretty and, most important, healthy. "This was just what I needed."

"Doctor knows best." That was why he'd suggested this. Her health.

Yeah, right.

He'd been counting the hours—minutes—until he could be with her. She was on his mind constantly when he was away from her. When he was with her, too. "I have a surprise for you."

She rose on her tiptoes. "I love surprises."

Her excitement pleased Cullen. Seeing her upset earlier with a life-as-she-knew-it-was-over expression on her face had made him feel as if he'd failed her somehow. He was relieved she was more like her old self, up for fun and adventure with him. "You'll like this one."

Friends greeted him from across the street. Cullen waved.

"Are you planning to stay in Hood Hamlet permanently?" Sarah asked.

"Yes," he said. "My lease on the cabin is up next month. I might sign another year lease or go month-to-month awhile. I'm considering buying a place."

"That's a big step."

True, but owning a house had always been part

of his plan. So had a wife and kids…. He glanced at Sarah and pushed the thought from his mind. "I like living here. It's a buyer's market."

"Strike while the iron is hot."

"Not quite." Cullen had learned his lesson by rushing into marriage. He jammed his hands into his jacket pockets. "I need to do more research first."

"What if you miss out on the perfect house?"

He'd thought Sarah was the perfect woman.

But that hadn't worked out the way he hoped. He didn't want to think about that today. "Then I'll wait for the next perfect place to come on the market."

Her gaze met his. "We're so different."

Understatement of the year. "We had some good times together in spite of our differences."

She nodded. "More good than bad."

Then why had she asked for a divorce? The question echoed through his head. But he knew the answer.

Sarah didn't love him. Oh, she'd never said those exact words when she'd brought up a divorce. She'd told him he deserved better. She'd told him to find another wife who could give him all he wanted.

All what? He'd had no idea what she'd been talking about. He'd wanted only her.

She glanced into the coffee shop. A customer exited. The scents of freshly baked cookies and coffee beans drifted out the open door. "No wonder every-one around here is so active. You need to burn off calories from all this delicious-smelling food."

"You figured out our motivation." Cullen played along. "The more time we spend on the mountain, the more we can eat without guilt."

"When have you ever felt guilty about eating?"

"At the hospital. When you couldn't," he admitted.

Sarah's gaze softened. "You're so sweet."

Brothers and friends were *sweet*. He would have preferred *hot* or *sexy*. But maybe that was where ex-husbands fitted in. He didn't much like the moniker. "Do you know where you want to settle?"

She shrugged. "I'm not sure I'm the settling type."

Not surprising. Sarah had always seemed to have a case of wanderlust. When she'd moved into his apartment in Seattle, everything she owned fitted in her car. "How much longer does your postdoc last?"

"It's hard to say after the accident. I estimate my funding will last a few more months, then I'll have to find a new position. I'm thinking about applying to the Global Volcano Monitoring Project."

The word *global* raised the hairs on the back of his neck. "What's that?"

"A nonprofit group that sends scientists all over the world, particularly to third-world nations, to set up volcano-monitoring systems and teach locals how to use them."

A sense of dread took root in his stomach. "Sounds interesting. Important."

She nodded. "It would be great experience and an adventure. I'd be able to do a lot of good."

"You would." So why did this sound like a bad idea to him? Maybe because he would never see her again. But they were getting a divorce. He wouldn't see her again no matter where she lived.

Cars passed by on the road. Neighbors greeted one another. A woman pushed a baby stroller. A tourist stood in the middle of the street snapping photographs.

"I see why you want to settle here," she said.

"Yeah." This was where Cullen wanted to be. So why couldn't he stop thinking about Sarah living in some remote village in Central America? He realized they'd reached their destination. He stopped and pointed to the wood plaque hanging from the building. "This is your surprise."

Sarah read the words written in gold script. "'Welton Wines and Chocolates.' Two of my favorite things."

"That's why I wanted to bring you here." Chocolate was the second-best way to get rid of Sarah's frustration. The first way was more fun, but not possible with her. He pulled his hand out of his pocket and opened the door. A bell tinkled, announcing their arrival. "After you."

Her eyes gleamed like emeralds. "Thank you."

He followed her inside. "You're welcome."

Warm air greeted Cullen, chasing away the cold. The aromas of chocolate and wine made his mouth water. The atmosphere was comfortable yet not too casual. Zoe Hughes had helped with the interior design. Chocolate was displayed to their left. A wine bar was on the right. In the back were black tables and chairs.

"This could be a dangerous place," Sarah whispered.

Not half as dangerous as her. "Let me have your coat."

Her eyes widened. "We're staying?"

"This wouldn't be much of a surprise if we walked in, turned around and left, now, would it?"

She grinned wryly. "I like your style, Dr. Gray."

Too bad Sarah hadn't liked him enough to stick with their marriage. No, that wasn't fair. Cullen bore responsibility for the breakup, too. He hung up their jackets on the hat tree by the door.

Christian Welton, a firefighter and Leanne's fiancé, shook his hand. "Good to see you, Doc."

"This is Sarah Purcell," Cullen said. "I wanted her to experience one of Owen's chocolate tastings."

"Great." The firefighter looked at Sarah. His easy smile widened. "I'm Christian Welton. Nice to meet you. Leanne's told me all about you."

Sarah's smile lit up her face. "Your ears should be burning. She said you were smokin' hot, and you are."

Leave it to Leanne and Sarah not to mince words.

Christian's cheeks reddened. "Leanne mentioned the two of you had a lot in common."

"You have no idea," Cullen said.

Sarah's lips pursed. "What's that supposed to mean?"

Christian's gaze met Cullen's in understanding. "It means you and Leanne keep us on our toes."

The bell on the door jingled. More customers entered.

"Take a seat." Christian motioned them to the tables in back. "We're getting set up. The tasting will begin soon."

Cullen and Sarah sat at a small round table sporting a single red rosebud in a glass vase and a lit votive candle. The flame flickered. Romantic. He hoped she liked this.

She looked around. "This is great."

The frown on her face didn't match her words. "You sure about that?"

"I'm a little confused. I thought Christian was a firefighter."

"He is, but his family owns a winery in the Willamette Valley," Cullen explained. "Christian and his cousin Owen opened this shop a few months ago and run it together. Owen is also a chocolatier."

She brightened. "That makes sense."

The bell on the door rang again. More people entered the shop, including Jake and Carly Porter and Hannah and Garrett Willingham, who sat at a table together.

Sarah waved. "Do you want to join your friends?"

Cullen wanted her all to himself. "This is fine."

Christian placed carafes of water, glasses and small plates of crackers on each of the tables. Next came paper place mats with squares numbered one through six and pencils for each taster. "Welcome to Welton Wines and Chocolate. Today we'll be doing a tasting with our chocolatier, Owen Welton Slayter."

Owen limped out from a back room, dressed in a white chef's jacket and gray pants. He also wore a leg brace, thanks to his climbing accident back in November. "Today we'll be tasting six samples, starting with milk chocolate that has the lowest percentage of cacao and ending with our darkest, most complex one. We've provided water at room temperature so it doesn't affect the chocolate or dull your taste buds and unsalted crackers to cleanse your palate between each sample."

"Is it a law all males must be attractive to live in Hood Hamlet?" Sarah whispered.

At least she still found him attractive. That pleased Cullen. "You'll have to ask the sheriff."

As Christian placed chocolate samples on the place mats, Owen lectured about the history of chocolate, beginning with the Mayans and Aztecs and the journey to Europe.

"This is in-depth." Sarah sounded impressed.

"Only the best for you, Lavagirl."

Her startled gaze met his.

Cullen understood her reaction. The words surprised him, too. But he meant them.

She opened her mouth to speak. "Cull—"

He touched his finger to her lips. So soft and smooth. Nothing like they'd been at the hospital. "Not now."

"Allow me to give you a few pointers about tasting chocolate," Owen said to the group. "Examine each sample. Look at the color and the texture. Smell it. Snap the sample in half. Does it sound sharp and crisp, soft and quiet or something in between? After you place the sample in your mouth, don't chew. Let the chocolate melt on your tongue so you can experience the flavors as they unfold. If you have any questions, just ask."

As Sarah looked at the place mat, her brows lowered.

Cullen scooted his chair closer to her. He wanted her to enjoy this, not be all tense and wary. "Let's have fun."

With a nod, she tasted sample number one, following Owen's instructions as if she were doing an experiment in the laboratory.

"What do you think?" Cullen whispered.

"This one is smooth, but I prefer a stronger chocolate."

He placed his arm around the back of her chair. "Mark what samples you like so we'll know what to buy later."

She tapped her pencil against the table. "Aren't you going to keep track of your favorites?"

Cullen didn't have to. He was looking at her now. "I'll keep track, too."

Amusement shone in her eyes. "Then you'd better taste your first selection or you'll be playing catch-up for the rest of the session."

He tasted the sample. "You're right. Not rich enough for me."

The next two had deeper flavors. Sarah decided

number three was the tastiest. She drew a heart around the number on her placement.

He toyed with the ends of her hair, letting the silky strands slip through his fingers. She glanced up at him, but didn't say a word. He took her silence as permission to continue.

"For centuries, many have touted the aphrodisiac qualities of chocolate," Owen lectured. "Some scientists have tried to debunk this, while others have claimed it's a psychological effect. Feel free to test this by feeding someone at your table sample number four."

Sarah held a chocolate in front of him with a hesitant look in her eyes. "Do you want me...?"

CHAPTER ELEVEN

CULLEN WANTED SARAH more than he could say. But he knew she wasn't asking *that* question. The chocolate would have to do. With a slight nod, he parted his lips.

She sucked in a breath. Her hand trembling, she brought the sample to his mouth.

He didn't know if she was nervous over him or because she was using her left hand. He hoped it wasn't the latter. He liked the idea she might be as affected by him as he was by her.

She carefully placed the chocolate onto his tongue. "What do you think?"

The intense flavor burst in his mouth with a nuttier and buttery taste. The third sample had been more velvety with a hint of orange.

"I like it." He picked up the fourth selection off his place mat. "Your turn."

Something resembling panic flashed in her eyes, but she opened her mouth anyway. He brought the chocolate closer. The tip of her tongue came out. Cullen fed her the sample.

Sarah's lips closed simultaneously with her eyes.

The aphrodisiac effects of chocolate might not be quantifiable, but he was feeling something. When she opened her eyes, the desire flaring in her gaze suggested she was feeling it, too.

He wanted to kiss her. Instead, he scribbled a star next to the number four on his place mat. "We're buying this one, too."

When he glanced back at Sarah, the tip of her tongue darted out once again and licked her lower lip.

Cullen wanted a taste. He leaned closer and kissed her. Gently.

She tensed for a moment, then relaxed and kissed him back. He pressed his lips harder against hers, enjoying the warmth, the sweetness and the touch of spice that was uniquely Sarah. As with the chocolate samples, the flavors unfolded one after another.

Her kiss filled the loneliness in his heart. He'd missed her so much. He didn't want her to go back to Bellingham or anywhere else.

"Let's move on to sample five," Owen said.

Cullen drew back, even if would rather have skipped the rest of the tasting and continued kissing her. The confusion in her eyes matched how he felt.

He'd kissed her. He'd been with her a large chunk of the day. And he hadn't felt himself losing control.

If anything, he was finding himself. He wanted to be a better husband, even if he wouldn't be one for much longer.

He marked his place mat with the pencil. "I'm going to want another taste of number seven."

Her eyebrows bunched. "There are only six samples."

"Seven, if I count you."

She smiled shyly at him through her eyelashes.

He leaned closer. "I have a strong feeling number seven is going to be my favorite."

Gratitude glistened in her eyes and something else. Something resembling...hope. "Mine, too."

The tasting continued. Cullen forced himself to concentrate. All he wanted to do was stare at Sarah and kiss her again. Not in that particular order. But she was paying attention to Owen, so Cullen did, too, while wondering how he could keep things going so well between them.

Number five was delicious with a coconut, sugary taste and went on the to-buy list. Number six was too bitter.

As the tasting came to an end, people discussed their observations. Everyone liked something different about the samples.

Cullen rubbed her back. "Enjoying yourself?"

"What are we doing?" she said in a low voice.

"Tasting chocolate."

"I mean…" She glanced around as if to see if any-one was listening. "You're acting like we're…"

"What?"

"Married."

"We are."

"For now." She glanced over at the table where his friends sat. "But you're doing all this lovey-dovey, couple stuff. I'll be honest. I'm enjoying it. But I'm sure your friends have noticed. What are they going to think?"

She enjoyed it. Good. Him, too. So much so he didn't want the lovey-dovey stuff, as she called it to end. "I don't care what they think."

"You said you told them about us."

He nodded. "They know I filed for divorce."

Sarah's face paled. "You filed?"

She sounded shocked. He moved his hand off her back, but kept his arm on her chair. "I mentioned I'd gotten things started when you were at the hospital."

She nibbled on her lip. "I'm sorry. You did, but I hadn't realized that meant you'd filed."

Okay, he was confused. What else would starting a divorce proceeding mean?

"No big deal who filed, right?" Except at the mo-ment, when all he wanted was to kiss her again, he was wondering if he'd been premature in setting the divorce into motion. "I hope you're not upset."

"Not upset." Her smile would have looked more natural on a mannequin. "I wasn't clear on what you meant. Probably the concussion."

"Probably." But doubts clamored to surface. Hope spread. In a flash, dreams and plans he'd long since suppressed surged to the forefront of his mind. His heart battered against his rib cage. "You still want a divorce, right?"

As soon as he'd spoken the words aloud, he regretted them, afraid to hear her answer. What if she said yes? What if she said no? Even if he wanted to try again, how could he ever trust she would want to stick around long-term? Especially with her life in Bellingham and his in Hood Hamlet. Logically divorce was the best—the only—option. And one of these days his heart would catch up to his head and agree.

It was taking her a long time to answer. Too long.

Cullen stood, disgusted with himself for thinking they might stand a chance. "I'm going to buy some chocolate while you think about it."

You still want a divorce, right?

If today was the benchmark for the future, then no, Sarah didn't. She tapped the pencil so fast against the table she might as well have picked up Cullen's and done a drum roll. But one day didn't make a marriage. Nor did two, the amount of time they'd spent together before eloping.

Even if things went well, how long would it be before Cullen realized he could do better or got tired of her and took off?

She dropped her pencil. Probably not long.

The sooner she could get out of here the better.

And she didn't mean this shop.

Carly walked up to the table with a big smile on her face. "It's so good to see you and Cullen here."

Hannah joined them. "I can't believe how much better you look. You're glowing."

"Thanks." Sarah didn't want to have to smile and make conversation with *Cullen's* friends who knew more about her marriage—make that the end of her marriage—than she did. But these women had become her friends, too. She could smile at them. And did. "The doctor's pleased with my progress."

Carly winked. "The good doctor seems very happy."

"The two of you look great together," Hannah said. "Seems like more is healing than your injuries."

Sarah pressed her toes into the ground so hard she was sure she'd split one of the floorboards. She understood these two women believed in a forever kind of love. They meant well, but she didn't know how to answer them. "Anything can happen."

She hoped that satisfied them.

"Especially here in Hood Hamlet," Hannah said.

Carly beamed. "Christmas magic in June."

Sarah had no idea what Carly was talking about. "Magic doesn't exist. It's nothing more than an illusion."

The two women shared a look.

"Of course you feel that way now. You're a scientist," Hannah said. "But after you've been in Hood Hamlet awhile, you'll change your mind."

Carly nodded. "It happens to everyone. Including Cullen."

Sarah remembered he'd mentioned Christmas magic when they'd arrived in town, but this was too woo-woo for her analytical brain. Magic no more existed than did everlasting love.

A good thing. She couldn't allow herself to be lured in by any yearning, whether it was to believe in magic or in love or a happily-ever-after. "I won't be in town long enough for that to happen."

"It doesn't look like Cullen's ready to send you back yet," Carly said.

Hannah nodded. "You have more healing to do."

"I do." But that wouldn't change her beliefs. She was a scientist grounded in fact. She had to stand firm. If she weren't careful, if she allowed herself to believe, her heart could be obliterated.

She glanced over at Cullen, wishing he would hurry so she could escape the scrutiny of his friends. But he was engrossed in a conversation with Jake, Garrett and Christian.

Cullen's gaze caught hers. The happiness in his eyes did painful things to her stomach that had nothing to do with her surgical incision or broken ribs. She struggled to breathe.

What was going on? The man had filed for divorce, and he still had this effect on her? A divorce she'd brought up, a little voice taunted.

Regret assailed her.

She looked back at the two women, who hadn't missed the exchange. Their enthusiastic smiles suggested they might think the divorce had been put on the back burner.

Sarah opened her mouth to clarify things, but no words came out.

This surprise was turning into a nightmare. She wanted to go home—strike that, back to the cabin—and hide away in her—the guest—bedroom until he had to go to work or on a mission.

Cullen walked over. He held up a white bag with gold lettering. "I've got the chocolate."

Good. Sarah could scarf down the entire bag once

she was in her room. She stood, eager to escape this place.

"I don't know if you have dinner plans for tonight, but we'd love for you to join us," Hannah said, much to Sarah's regret. "Jake and Carly are coming over with Nicole, so this will be a kid-friendly menu. Nothing fancy, just lasagna."

"Sarah loves lasagna," Cullen said.

She was touched he remembered and annoyed he'd bring it up now. She forced a feeble smile.

"I'm bringing dessert," Carly added.

Cullen looked at Sarah. "What do you say?"

Darn him. He'd left the decision up to her. Sure, she had an easy out if she said she was tired. People would understand. Too bad she was confused and wary and apprehensive, but not tired. How could she lie to a woman who had done so much to care for her? "Sure, sounds fun."

As much fun as more surgery.

Hannah grinned. "Great."

Yes, great. At least Hannah was happy. Sarah's face muscles hurt trying to keep her panic from showing, but her smile never wavered. She had a feeling this would be a long evening. At least she had one of Carly's desserts to look forward to at the end. And Sarah realized there was one bright spot ahead—she wouldn't be spending the evening alone with Cullen.

She tugged on her ear. Maybe dinner out wasn't such a bad idea after all.

"The lasagna was great, Hannah." Cullen enjoyed being at the Willinghams' house. Nothing like sitting at a crowded dinner table with good friends, tasty food and his beautiful wife. His arm rested on her chair. The ends of her hair tickled his skin with each turn of her head. He could get used to this. "Thanks for inviting us over."

"Everything was so delicious," Sarah agreed, as did Jake and Carly.

Cullen's thigh touched Sarah's. He thought about shifting positions to break the contact, but she wasn't scooting away. Might as well stay put, even if his blood was simmering.

He wished it could always be like this with Sarah. Hanging out with other couples. Kids running around.

Going out with others was something they'd never done in Seattle. With such busy schedules, they'd kept to themselves, spending any free time with each other. Maybe that had been a mistake.

Hannah wiped the mouth of her two-year-old son, Tyler. The boy squirmed and scrunched up his face.

She didn't miss a beat. "Would you like dessert now or later?"

"Later," all the adults said at the same time.

"Then let's go into the living room," Hannah said. "Cleanup can wait."

Garrett leaned over and kissed his wife. "I'll take care of it for you."

Her older children—Kendall and Austin—bolted from the table. Tyler and fifteen-month-old Nicole, Jake and Carly's daughter, toddled after them, nearly crashing into each other twice.

Carly laughed. "At least diapers provide padding when they fall."

The adults followed the kids into the living room and took seats on the worn but comfortable furniture. Pieces from a jigsaw puzzle covered the coffee table. Crayons and Lego lay scattered on the floor.

This was the kind of house Cullen wanted to buy. Warm and cozy, well-built and designed for a family. But his dreams about having a family had always included Sarah. Never any other woman, only her.

She sat on the couch with Carly.

He wished Sarah had sat by him on the loveseat instead.

The two women joked about something wedding-related.

He understood why Sarah had wanted to elope

after being jilted on her wedding day, but he'd never asked if she wanted a reception or a party to celebrate their marriage. They'd never taken a honeymoon, only short climbing trips. They'd never shared a bank account, either.

Framed photographs covered the fireplace mantel. The wedding pictures drew his gaze. He and Sarah had two wedding photographs, one with the Elvis impersonator and one of the two of them. It had seemed enough at the time. And too much when he'd been moving out.

Jake and Garrett fiddled with the stereo until music played.

A picture of a climber standing atop Mount Hood with a big grin on his face caught Cullen's attention. The gear, over ten years old, dated the photo. That must be Nick Bishop, Carly's brother, Hannah's first husband and Kendall and Austin's dad, who'd died in a climbing accident on Mount Hood.

The women laughed over something borrowed. Or was it blue?

Kendall, who was around twelve, carried in a cardboard box and set it at Sarah's feet. "My mom says you're a volcano scientist."

"I am," Sarah said enthusiastically. "At Mount Baker Volcano Institute. My specialty is seismology."

The girl's face fell. "Bummer. I need someone to help me who knows something about lava flow."

The corners of Sarah's mouth twitched, but she kept a serious expression on her face. "I know something about lava. What do you need help with?"

"My science-fair project."

Hannah touched her daughter's thin shoulder. "Sarah is a guest. Let's not bother her with your homework."

Kendall shrugged away from her mother's hand. "But you and dad know nothing about volcanoes."

"I'm happy to help," Sarah said, much to Cullen's surprise, given her pensive mood and how inexperienced she seemed to be around kids. "I've given some talks at schools and led geology field trips around Mount Baker."

As Kendall dug through the box, Hannah mouthed the words *thank you* to Sarah. Austin showed Jake his newest hand-held video game. Carly played peek-a-boo with Nicole and Tyler. Garrett adjusted the stereo volume.

Sarah gave Hannah a quick nod, then focused on Kendall. "Let me see what you have."

The girl showed her the box jam-packed with maps, a plastic bucket and other things Cullen couldn't quite recognize.

"Looks like you've got plenty to make a project,"

Sarah said. "Is there a quieter place where we can work?"

"Yes. I know just the place." Kendall, all limbs and hair, scrambled to her feet. "Follow me."

As Kendall jogged out of the living room carrying her box with her little brother Tyler chasing after her, Sarah stood. "How much help is Kendall allowed to have with the project?"

"She's supposed to do the majority of the physical work herself," Garrett said. "But she can have as much assistance as needed with the concepts and science behind the project."

"Got it," Sarah said.

"Tyler went back with Kendall. If he's in the way, let me know," Garrett added.

Sarah waved her hand. "No worries. We'll find something for him to do."

Her willingness to help surprised Cullen, given her awkwardness with his nephews and nieces during that Easter. Maybe spending more time with kids on field trips had made a difference. He remembered what she'd said to him during their conversation in his living room.

I wanted to help with dinner. I tried to help. But I only got in their way. They kicked me out of the kitchen and told me to go find you.

Had his family treated Sarah the same way when

it came to the kids? Granted, they hadn't been happy when he'd eloped because they worried his behavior had been too reckless. But surely his family wouldn't have taken their concerns out on Sarah.

Except that was what he'd done, he realized with regret. He'd blamed Sarah for his impulsive behavior in Las Vegas. Even though it had made him feel better, happy, complete.

Hannah stared down the hallway. "Sarah doesn't have to do this."

"She knows that," Cullen explained. "But given the choice between volcanoes and doing something else, she'll pick volcanoes every time."

But the words didn't quite ring true to him. She'd had research to do with her dissertation and other obligations at the university. But she'd worked around his schedule as much as possible. He hadn't felt like a priority because he hadn't wanted to be one. He'd wanted her to be busy so he had reason to be busy, too. Busy…distracted. He rubbed the back of his neck.

Carly picked up Nicole. "You know, the USGS Cascade Volcano Observatory isn't that far away."

Jake held a bottle of beer. "Vancouver, Washington, isn't exactly close."

"It's closer than Bellingham, where Sarah works now," Hannah countered.

Garrett shot his wife a pointed look. Something Cullen hadn't expected from the button-downed CPA who was also OMSAR's treasurer. "Drop it."

Jake nodded. "You, too, Carly. Doc doesn't need you interfering in his life."

"Especially his marriage," Garrett added.

"What? We haven't done anything." Hannah raised her palms. "Carly and I thought we'd mention it in case Cullen and Sarah want to be closer."

Closer, huh? The muscle cords in Cullen's neck tightened. Sarah had been right. His friends had noticed what was going on at the chocolate tasting and had made their own assumptions. Wrong ones. Though a part of him wished they were correct. Sarah had never answered his question about still wanting the divorce. "Sarah and I aren't back together."

"Not yet anyway." Carly spoke as if she knew a big secret. "Anyone can see the two of you are perfect together."

He'd thought that once himself. Now...

Jake blew out an exasperated breath. "Be careful, Doc, or you'll find these two playing matchmaker."

Hannah placed her hands on her hips. "We aren't that bad."

"That's because you haven't been given the chance," Garrett said. "They mean well, Doc, but don't let them get away with anything or you'll have an avalanche on your hands."

Cullen gave both men a nod. He stood. "Appreciate the warning, gentlemen. I'm going to see how the science project is coming along."

And get out from under the would-be-matchmaking reach of the ladies.

"Just follow the sounds of wailing and gnashing of teeth and you'll find Kendall," Hannah said.

Carly made a sour face. "Hey, that's my niece you're talking about."

"Wait until Nicole turns twelve," Hannah said. "You'll understand. I can't imagine what it'll be like when she turns thirteen."

Cullen left them to discuss teenagers. Walking down the hallway, he didn't hear any wailing, but a few giggles and squeals pierced the quiet. He followed the sounds until he came to a garage.

He stood in the doorway.

The three sat on the concrete floor with the contents of the box spread out in front of them. Tyler played with an empty toilet paper roll. He couldn't seem to make up his mind whether it was a sword or a bugle.

"This is going to be so cool." Kendall knelt, leaning forward with an excited gleam in her eyes. "If it works."

"It'll work." Sarah pointed to a piece of paper on the floor. "You need to attach this onto the topographic map."

"Like this," the girl said shyly.

Sarah gave Kendall the thumbs-up sign. "That's perfect."

Tyler mimicked the action.

Grinning at the little boy, Sarah pulled him onto her lap. "You are too cute."

The boy gazed up at her with pure adoration.

Cullen's heart stuttered.

As Tyler examined her cast, Sarah touched Kendall's shoulder. "You're doing an excellent job."

Kendall beamed. "That's because I have you."

"You're doing all the work." Sarah sounded like a mom.

Cullen couldn't breathe.

"I'm simply your scientific adviser," she added.

"Is it fun being a scientist?" Kendall asked.

Sarah's beaming smile hit Cullen like a blast from a laser gun. He leaned against the doorjamb to keep from falling on his ass. Because that was the next place he'd be. No doubt about it.

"Being a scientist is the most fun job in the world," she said, and explained what she did at MBVI.

Kendall held on to Sarah's every word. He didn't blame the girl. He was the same way.

"Is it better than being a wife and mom?" Kendall asked.

Sarah's tender gaze washed over the two children. "I don't have kids, so I don't know about that, but being a wife can be fun, too."

Cullen listened in disbelief, held spellbound by the woman he'd married. His life plan swirled inside his brain, reconfiguring and amending itself by the second.

Kendall fiddled with a piece of plastic. "I can use water for the lava."

"You could, but molasses would work better due to its viscosity."

"My mom has molasses in the pantry." Kendall looked up at Sarah. "But I'm not sure what *visc...* whatever word you said means."

"Viscosity."

Kendall repeated the word. "Viscosity."

Sarah nodded. "Viscosity is the measure of a fluid's resistance to flow."

"Huh?"

"Imagine you have a cup of water and a cup of honey. Which drains faster?"

"The water. Honey moves slower."

"That's right," Sarah said. "Honey has a higher viscosity than water, so it resists flow more. Same with molasses."

"Makes sense."

As the two worked on the volcano, Cullen was captivated by how much Sarah had changed from being awkward and uncomfortable around his family at Easter to at ease with Tyler and Kendall.

This different side, this new side of Sarah appealed to him at a gut level. He pictured her with children of her own, nurturing them, mothering them. All the heady dreams he'd had when they'd first married rushed to the forefront of his mind. Sarah pregnant with his child. A girl with her laugh. A boy with her sharp wit. They would be a family.

His family.

Cullen's heart ached with yearning so strong he started walking toward Sarah. Until he realized she would be the mom of some other guy's kids.

He balled his hands.

You still want a divorce, right?

She hadn't answered him, but that didn't matter. Forget pride. Forget everything.

He didn't want to lose her, but how could he convince her to give their marriage another shot? What if she didn't want to try again?

His heart thudded. But what if she did?

CHAPTER TWELVE

Cullen unlocked the front door of the cabin. "You were amazing tonight."

Sarah walked inside. She wanted to be unaffected by him, yet all she wanted to do was kiss him. She couldn't give in to her impulsive side. Not with her heart at stake. "I didn't do that much."

"You only made a kid's night by helping her put together what will be the winning science project."

Sarah had never felt like such a part of a community, of a family, until tonight. She'd loved every single second of being at the Willinghams' house, from eating dinner to helping Kendall with her volcano model to holding Tyler with his ever-sticky hands. For the first time in Sarah's life she'd wondered if she could be a good wife and mother in spite of her past.

Sadness trembled down her spine. Too bad Hood Hamlet wasn't her community. She would never have a family with Cullen here. She swallowed a sigh. "Anyone would have helped."

"But you did."

She shrugged off her jacket. "I don't know why you're making such a big deal about this."

"The last time you were around kids, you looked like you wanted to run and hide."

Easter. The right sleeve got caught on her cast.

Cullen removed it for her. He hung the jacket on the hat tree by the door. "Tonight was the antithesis of that."

Sarah crossed her left arm over her chest and rubbed her cast. "Tonight was more real than Easter with your family."

With his hand at the small of her back, he led her into the living room. "Easter was real."

She sat on the couch, and he sat next to her. "Okay, it was real, but everything was scheduled with military precision. We moved from one thing to the next without having a chance to enjoy the moment. No chance to catch our breaths. No time to think about anything. I understand now that's the whole purpose of the holiday being so over-the-top. The day is so jam-packed with things Blaine doesn't have a chance to enter your minds."

He rubbed his palms on his thighs as if drying them off. "I told you it's a coping mechanism."

"Yes. But remember, I hadn't a clue then." She needed to get this out, if only for her peace of mind. "All I saw were little kids who wanted to play with their Easter baskets and eat candy, not do crafts, be forced into organized games and march in a parade. I mentioned it to your mom, who snapped at me. Your sisters jumped all over me, too."

His nostrils flared. "Why didn't you tell me?"

"You never wanted to talk about anything." Sarah kept her voice low and steady, even though her emotions and stomach churned. "Why would this be any different?"

"I…" He hung his head. "It's probably too late to apologize."

Sarah touched his hand; his skin was rough and calloused and warm. "It's okay. Addiction does crazy things to people, and this is how your family deals with what happened to Blaine. But it would have been easier knowing going in, and it would have saved a lot of heartache."

He nodded. "I'm not one for doing a lot of talking."

"You had no problem talking to me in Las Vegas."

"Vegas was different."

"Yes, it was." Those two days had been a fairy tale. But once back in the real world, they couldn't sustain the fantasy. "It was easy there. We could be what each other needed. Back in Seattle, not so much."

His eyes darkened to a midnight-blue. "That's—"

"The truth."

Cullen didn't say anything, but his chin dropped.

A nod of agreement? She couldn't be sure.

"We're been doing better now," he said. "Talking. Trying."

"Yes, but this isn't real. I mean, I'm still recovering. It's almost like I'm on vacation."

"Like in Red Rocks."

Disappointment squeezed her heart. She nodded. "But you're not on vacation. You're home. I realized Hood Hamlet's real appeal to you tonight."

Cullen's gaze met hers.

Sarah's pulse skittered.

"What's that?" he asked.

"The community, the people. They're one big extended family. You take care of one another and have each other's backs, like your sisters had your mom's with me. Or Leanne wanting to know about our marriage."

"Or Hannah and Carly mentioning the volcano observatory in Vancouver wasn't that far away."

Sarah's mouth gaped. "They didn't."

"They sure did." Cullen sounded amused. "Much to Garrett and Jake's dismay."

"No wonder you found your way back to the kids and me."

"I was afraid to stay in the living room any longer." She laughed.

"Maybe I should have listened to what they had

to say. Because they're right about one thing." He raised her hand to his mouth and kissed it. "You belong here."

Her heart stumbled.

"In Hood Hamlet," he continued.

Sarah thought he was going to say with him. Hoped he would. But he didn't. She ignored the disappointment. "I live in Bellingham. MBVI is there."

"I live here." He faced her, his gaze trapping hers. "We should be together."

The poles shifted. Her world spun off its axis. Air rushed from her lungs. "Together?"

He nodded with a determined set to his jaw. "A couple."

Surprise clogged her throat. It took a second to find her voice. "We already tried that."

"We're good together."

"Sometimes."

"That's a start."

If only… No. Too much separated them. Too high a wall to climb, too wide a river to cross. "We're too different."

A seductive fire blazed in his eyes. "Opposites attract."

He leaned closer. His heat enveloped her.

She felt light-headed. "They can also repel."

One side of his mouth lifted in a sexy grin. "We definitely attract."

She struggled to breathe.

"I'll prove it to you." His lips swooped down on her. He kissed her hard until her toes curled, sparks ignited under her skin and she was gasping for air. "Enough of a data point, or do you need more?"

Oh, she had all the information she needed to make a conclusion. That brief but oh-so-hot kiss reminded her of the time they'd first met. His kisses had stripped her bare, leaving her naked and emotionally vulnerable and wanting another kiss. All her dormant fairy-tale fantasies had clamored to be heard.

But Sarah didn't need to be rescued. She couldn't fall under Cullen's spell the way she had in Las Vegas. The way he'd—they'd—been acting tonight made it so easy to believe they could be a couple again, not the same as before, but like Hannah and Garrett or Carly and Jake. The way Sarah had always dreamed.

But how long would that last?

Her parents had abandoned her. Dylan, her ex-fiancé, too. She found it hard—okay, impossible—to believe Cullen would stay the distance. And when he left her...

She couldn't let him make her believe in magic or happy endings. "I can't."

He stroked her cheek with his knuckle. "You're going to have to give me more than that."

That was what she was afraid he would say. "I'm tired."

He wrapped a finger around a loose curl. "We can have this conversation lying down."

Warning bells clanged in her head. "Cullen."

"Nothing wrong with the horizontal position," he said. "You used to like it."

Loved it. Heat pooled low in her belly and spread outward, making her limbs feel like liquid silver. She swallowed.

"Come on." He pulled her up from the couch and tugged her gently forward by a wayward curl. "Get ready for bed. Then you can tell me why you 'can't.'"

Can't. Can't. Can't. The word echoed through Sarah's head.

She was tired, but took her time in the bathroom. A mix of procrastination and nerves, each vying for victory. But she didn't imagine there would be any winners tonight.

Apprehension coursed through her veins. She put her robe on over her pajamas. An extra layer of protection. Not from Cullen. From herself.

In her room she crawled into bed, then pulled the covers to her neck. She willed herself to sleep. Hard to talk if she was asleep.

Cullen entered the room wearing only pajama bottoms. His muscular arms and smooth chest and his defined abs made her mouth water. He looked as though he'd been sculpted to her specifications.

She itched to run her fingers over his skin, to feel his strength and his warmth. To have his hands touch her all over.

Sarah shivered with need.

He took a step toward her.

"I'm not having sex with you." The words fell from her mouth like a glacier calving.

His lopsided, sexy grin appeared again. "Who said anything about having sex?"

The man was sex with a stethoscope. Well, if he had one with him. "Just setting some ground rules."

"That's rule number one. Any more?"

She narrowed her gaze. "Maybe."

Laughter sparkled in his eyes. He turned off the light.

Darkness filled the room. She couldn't see or hear him. As he stretched out beside her, the mattress dipped.

She tightened her grip on the blanket. "Stay on top of the covers."

"Your wish is my command."

Sarah gulped. That was what she was afraid of. Because she wanted him. Now. Here in his house. In this bed.

He cuddled against her.

Every muscle tensed. "What are you doing?"

"Getting comfortable for our conversation."

That would be impossible for her to do. Even with the covers, a robe and pajamas separating them, she felt the warmth emanating from his body. And it felt good.

"So why can't we be together?" he asked.

"You're serious about having this discussion in bed?"

"You sound surprised," he said. "Did you think I was going to put the moves on you?"

"Yes." She'd hoped. And dreaded. And, well, she was about as confused as she could be right now.

He guffawed. "O, ye of little faith."

"I have only past experience to go by." She inhaled, then exhaled slowly. "That's why I can't be with you. I'm no good at relationships."

Sarah expected him to offer up a counterpoint. He didn't. The crushing weight of disappointment settled on her chest.

The house creaked. The heater came on, shooting warm air through the vents. Outside the wind blew.

He brushed his fingers through her hair. "Why do you think that?"

She doubted he wanted to stay up all night to hear the long list of reasons. Might as well cut to the chase. "I haven't told you much about my parents."

"You said they've each been divorced multiple times and they're no longer part of your life."

Sarah remembered the last time she saw her mother. It still hurt to think about. "I was an only child, and my parents should have never had me. I think they regretted it. But one thing was clear. They didn't care about me."

"What do you mean?"

"They never wanted me around. After the divorce, they shuttled me back and forth."

He pulled her closer. "That's no way to treat a child."

"No, but that's what they did." The numb tone of her voice matched the way she felt. Resigned. Indifferent. That was how she wanted to feel about what had happened. "I've never seen a successful relationship or experienced one. Only broken ones."

"You saw two tonight at dinner."

"A glimpse." She shivered, and his arms tightened around her. "Being jilted and having my parents walk away has skewed my view."

"You don't have to tell me."

"I want to." She should have told him long ago. "I wanted you to talk to me, but I wasn't so eager to do the same myself."

"We both share the blame. I didn't ask you a lot of questions," he admitted. "So your folks…"

"My mom's fourth husband made a pass at me. It's something that had happened before with men she was dating, so I always kept myself scarce so I wouldn't get hurt, but it had never happened with one of my stepfathers."

Cullen brushed his lips over her hair. "I'm sorry it had to happen at all."

"I told my mom because I was scared, but my stepfather lied. Claimed I was trying to seduce him. My mom believed him and kicked me out of the house. It was heartbreaking, humiliating, you name it."

The memory burned through her.

"Shame on your mom. That's horrible for choosing a man over her own daughter." He squeezed her. "Did you go live with your dad?"

"Yes, but I bounced around a lot. I was still in high school. I ended up spending a lot of time with Dylan."

"You were with him a long time."

She nodded. "He was all I had. When I turned eighteen, my dad remarried again. His new wife, Caylee, was uncomfortable having a stepdaughter who was just four years younger than her. After I graduated high school, I never saw my dad again."

"Sarah—"

"It's okay. I ended up with a pair of not-so-great parents, but at least they didn't beat me."

"They did in other ways." His warm breath caressed her neck. "I can't believe I'm saying this, but it's good they're out of your life. Neither deserves a daughter like you."

And she didn't deserve Cullen. Because he needed someone who knew how to make relationships work. She didn't.

Tears stung her eyes. Sarah blinked them away.

"But you're not destined to repeat what your rotten parents did," he said. "You can have what they've never had—good, solid relationships. Ones that last."

"Maybe I can do better than my parents." But no way would any relationship last. The result would be the same. She would end up alone and brokenhearted. The way she always had. "But I've learned my lesson. I can't jump back into something…"

"That something is our marriage."

"You know what I mean."

"I do," he said. "But here's the deal. We don't have to jump back into anything. We did that the first time around. It didn't work. There's nothing to stop us from going slower this time."

A vise tightened around her heart. "I'm not going to be here much longer. We don't live in the same state."

"Long distance can't be any worse than being apart for the past year."

A flutter of hope emerged. "I suppose that's true."

"It is true. But don't decide right now," he said to her relief. "Think about it. Think about what it'll take to turn your 'I can't' into an 'I want to.' Will you do that for me? For us?"

Affection for Cullen deepened. He might have been a stranger when they got married, but she'd picked a great guy to marry even if he had a few faults. "Yes, I will."

He squeezed her shoulder. "Now get some sleep."

She wanted him next to her all night. "Will you stay, please?"

"You're going to have to kick me out. Though I can't promise you I won't sneak under the covers if it gets colder."

"You can get under them now."

"Let's not test my self-control too much." He kissed her forehead. "Sweet dreams, Lavagirl."

Sheltered in his arms, Sarah had a feeling she would have very sweet dreams. Maybe a couple of hot ones, too, starring the handsome and incredibly fit Dr. Gray. She hoped she woke up knowing the answer to his question.

What would it take to turn her "I can't" to "I want to"?

The next day, Cullen put away the dishes while Sarah looked at the newest data from Mount Baker. Everything she'd told him last night tumbled around in his head. He couldn't believe they'd been married and knew so little about each other.

I've never seen a successful relationship or experienced one. Only broken ones.

He ached for her. But he needed to know stuff like that if they wanted their marriage to work. Sarah needed help. Therapy, perhaps, maybe together the way his family had done. That could help her move forward so they could work things out. If she wanted to work things out…

All he could do now was wait and hope.

The next two days passed quickly. Too quickly for Sarah. She had no idea what to say to Cullen. Fortunately, he'd been working at the hospital and on a ready team, so she could avoid the confrontation. But she couldn't put it off much longer.

Rays of morning sunlight streamed in the kitchen window. Sarah made herself a cup of chamomile tea. Cullen sat at the kitchen table reading the paper. Today was the beginning of three days off for him. He was looking forward to it. She had mixed feelings. "Want something to drink?"

He lofted a smile her way. "No, thanks. But I'll take another blueberry muffin. Then maybe we could talk."

She picked up a muffin for him, but nerves made her almost drop it. If Christmas magic did exist, in June or December or whenever, she wished it could come to the rescue now.

He glanced over the paper at her. "Sean invited us to a BBQ tomorrow night. Everyone will be there. I went ahead and told him we'd attend."

She hoped people wouldn't want to talk about her and Cullen. But given the phone calls after the dinner at the Willinghams' house, she knew the chances of that were slim to none.

Her cell phone beeped with a text message.

"Must be Tucker," she said. "He's early this morning."

"Tell him you're still recovering, if he wants you back."

"I'm nearly self-sufficient now."

His gaze locked on hers. "You ready to go back?"

"No."

With a little smirk, he returned to reading the paper.

Sarah's cell phone rang. Tucker's ring tone. That was odd. Considering the text was most likely from him.

She walked to the recliner, picked up her phone and saw the words *Steam Blast* on the screen. Her heart slammed against her chest. Forcing herself to breathe, she hit the answer button. "What's happening up there?"

CHAPTER THIRTEEN

SARAH'S WHITE-KNUCKLE grip on the phone, her stiff posture and the rise in her voice told Cullen all he needed to know. It was time for her to go. A weight pressed down on his chest, right over his heart.

She disconnected the call.

He took a deep breath. "Tucker wants you back."

"Another steam burst occurred this morning." She gathered her papers and shoved them into her laptop bag. "Tucker needs me there. Now."

No. The word positioned itself on the tip of Cullen's tongue ready to spring out into the world. Sarah couldn't go to Bellingham. She wasn't healed enough. Not exactly true, but he would do or say whatever he had to in order to make her stay. He wasn't ready to let her go. If she went away, she might not come back. Especially with things so up in the air between them. "Now?"

"Tucker would have preferred having me there yesterday, but since we don't have a time machine handy..."

Cullen's cell phone vibrated. He pulled it from his pocket to turn it off. He glanced at the screen.

Damn. A rescue-mission call out. "I don't believe this."

She stopped her flurry of activity. "What?"

"Missing climbers."

Someone needed help on the mountain, but Sarah needed help here. Priorities waged battle against loyalty. He had a duty—two actually. The physician and mountain rescuer wanted to be part of the mission, to help whoever was in need. The husband wanted to be with his wife because he might not have much time left with her.

Cullen stood. "The unit's gathering at Timberline Lodge, but I can skip this one and drive you to Bellingham."

"You're needed on the rescue."

He could be. "I don't know the mission specifics. It might not be anything. I've missed missions when I was in the middle of a shift and couldn't get someone to cover for me. They'll have plenty of rescuers."

"You're the only doctor."

His throat thickened. "I'm driving you."

Their gazes locked. Neither moved or said a word. Stalemate.

"How long will your mission take?" she asked finally.

"I don't know."

She wrapped her fingers around her laptop. "What if I wait until you get back? I need to pack all my things. I can look at data here until you return."

His heart swelled with relief, gratitude and affection. "That would be wonderful. I'll be back as soon as I can."

"Don't rush on my account." Concern clouded her gaze. "Please be careful."

He wanted to wipe the worry away, wanted to take her in his arms and hold her close, wanted to tell her how much her waiting meant to him. Instead, he kissed her lightly on the lips, forcing himself not to take the kiss deeper. But he'd make up for it...later. "Always. We don't take needless risks up there."

The pink tip of her tongue darted out and moistened her lips. "I'm holding you to that."

He wanted to run his tongue along her lips. Hell, he wanted to taste her all over. *No time now.* "Please do."

His gear was packed due to an upcoming ready team, but he double-checked the equipment. He filled his thermos. "I'll have someone check on you."

"Thanks, but there's no need. I've been through this when you were with the rescue group in Seattle. I'll be fine. As long as I know..."

"Know what?"

Sarah's tender gaze washed over him. "That you're safe."

Her words tugged at his heart. Cullen didn't want to leave her. He didn't want her to leave him. "Rescuer safety is priority number one. Our mission plans are built around that."

"I know." Sarah didn't sound convinced.

He didn't want her to worry about him. "If you don't want me to go—"

"Go." She cut him off. "I'm being…silly."

He ran his index finger along her jawline. "You're pretty cute when you're silly."

She stuck her tongue out at him.

Cullen laughed. If only it could always be like this. But she was needed in Bellingham. For now. Maybe not for long. Her postdoc position wouldn't last forever. He kissed her forehead. "Pack your things. I'll be back before you know it."

When he arrived home, he would tell her that she always had a place here with him. That he hoped she would return soon. That he hoped she would want to stay. Because he wanted her with him. He hoped she felt the same way.

At two o'clock, snow fell from the darkening sky. Sarah couldn't believe another storm was hitting in

June. Especially with three climbers missing and rescue teams searching for them.

More data downloaded from MBVI's server. Tucker wasn't happy she wasn't on her way, but she was doing all she could from here.

She pressed her cheek against the window. The cold stung her skin, but she kept her face there. Cullen had to be freezing wherever he was. Wet, too. She prayed he was okay.

The doorbell rang.

Sarah jumped. Maybe Cullen had finished with the mission. She hurried to open the door.

A woman in her forties with short curly hair stood on the front porch. "I'm looking for Sarah Purcell."

Brrr. It was colder than Sarah had realized. Goose bumps covered her skin. "I'm she."

"I have a delivery from this company." The woman pointed to the name Haskell, Thayer & Henry printed on a large white envelope, then handed it to Sarah. "Please sign this acceptance of service acknowledging you received the papers."

Sarah tucked the envelope under her arm. She scribbled her signature.

The woman thanked her and walked toward her car.

Sarah backed into the cabin, as if moving in slow motion. Her fingers gripped the envelope. She didn't need to open it to know what was inside. Well, she was 99.99 percent certain.

I knew you were busy, so once I established residency in Oregon I got things started there.

They know I filed for divorce.

Divorce papers. Her stomach roiled. Sarah thought she might be sick. Okay, he'd filed before her accident, but it still hurt.

Sarah plodded into the kitchen and placed the envelope on the breakfast bar. She'd wait until Cullen returned to open it. She had too much to worry about, with him on the mountain in a storm and the second steam blast on Mount Baker.

Hours passed. Sarah looked at data and spoke with Tucker over Skype. But what she wanted was to hear from Cullen. A phone call. A text.

The doorbell rang.

She was almost afraid to answer the door again, but she did. The wind whipped. Snow fell in a solid sheet of white. Carly, Zoe and Christian Welton stood on the porch, bundled up in parkas and hats.

Sarah invited them in. She assumed Cullen had asked his friends to check on her. She was glad he'd done that even though she'd told him not to. She needed the company. "I can't believe you three ventured out in this kind of weather."

"We wanted to see how you were doing." Zoe removed her hat, scarf, coat and mittens, then hung them on the hat tree. "We also have some news."

Sarah forced herself not to hold her breath. "Good news, I hope."

Carly hung her coat. "Rescue Team 4 found the missing climbers and brought them down."

Relief flowed through Sarah, loosening her tense muscles. "That's wonderful. Everyone will be home soon."

Forget about the divorce papers. Sarah wiggled her toes with anticipation. She wanted to see Cullen.

"Almost everyone," Christian said. "Teams 2 and 3 are stuck on the mountain. They'll be down once there's a break in the weather."

"Is Cullen on one of those teams?" she asked.

Carly nodded. "Sean, Jake, Bill, Tim and Cullen are hunkering down in a snow cave. They're fine, but the conditions are pretty bad up there."

The hair on Sarah's arms stood on end. That didn't sound good at all.

"The guys made the smart decision, given the conditions," Christian said. "Leanne and the rest of Team 3 made it to the Palmer lift station before the whiteout made it too dangerous for them to continue. They'll stay there tonight."

Worried, Sarah chewed on her lower lip.

"Everyone is fine," Carly reiterated. "But staying put will keep them safe tonight."

Sarah had slept in a snow cave, part of an alpine mountaineering course she'd taken. A snow cave would protect the team from the elements. That was crucial in this kind of weather. But she would rather have Cullen home.

Zoe raised a paper sack. "We brought dinner."

"No reason to sit alone when we're all in the same boat," Christian explained.

Carly nodded. "We stopped by Tim's place, but Rita and Wyatt are at her parents' house in Portland. The other guys on Rescue 3 live down the mountain."

Sarah appreciated their thoughtfulness. Food was the last thing on her mind, but she needed to eat. To keep up her strength. She wanted to be strong for Cullen. "Thanks. This is so nice of you."

Carly touched Sarah's arm. "It's good for all of us."

"Where's Nicole?" Sarah asked.

"With Hannah and Graham," Carly said. "Jake and I were supposed to have a date night."

"Skip the barbecue tomorrow night and go on your date instead," Zoe suggested.

Carly hugged Zoe. "Thanks, but we'll find another night to go out."

As the four of them prepared dinner, Sarah realized in the short time she'd been in Hood Hamlet, she'd made good friends. Some of that was due to her job, but part—a big part—was the change in her. She didn't let people get close. In Hood Hamlet, that didn't stop people from butting their noses into her life anyway. Maybe that wasn't such a bad thing.

Zoe set the table. "I'm happy we're doing this tonight. When I'm at the base helping out, I'm not so impatient. But I hate waiting."

"Me, too." Sarah would give anything to touch Cullen right now. "I really wish it would stop snowing."

"Rescuer safety is the priority when they're on a mission," Zoe explained. "Sean tells me that over and over again."

Carly nodded. "Jake, too."

Christian prepared chicken marsala. "Add Leanne to the list."

Sarah sighed. "Cullen said the same thing to me."

Zoe placed napkins at each of the four place settings. "What they don't seem to understand is no matter what the conditions are, it's hard not to worry when the love of your life is up on the mountain."

Sarah nodded in agreement.

Wait a minute.

The love of her life? Cullen?

Truth scorched like the hot lava from Kilauea in Hawaii.

Oh, no. She wasn't falling for Cullen. She'd fallen.

She loved him. Truly loved him. With all her heart, body and soul.

What had she done? She folded her left arm over her stomach.

Zoe rushed to Sarah's side. "You're so pale. Sit."

She sat.

Christian knelt, taking her pulse. "Does anything hurt?"

"No." Her voice cracked.

Carly touched Sarah's forehead with the back of her hand. "You don't feel warm."

"I'm not sick." Not unless you wanted to count being lovesick. "Give me a minute. I'm a little light-headed."

A worried look passed between Carly and Christian. His forehead wrinkled. "Put your head between your legs."

Sarah did. She hated making her friends worry when the problem wasn't her injuries. But what could she say to them? That she'd just realized she loved her husband? Loved him to the point nothing else mattered?

"Feel better?" Carly asked.

"Yes."

Physically Sarah did. But emotionally...

This was the worst thing ever. Loving Cullen gave him complete power over her, to hurt her when he no longer wanted her. And he wouldn't want her to be with him forever. How could he? No one else had.

Building a volcano and playing with a toddler didn't mean she would be a good mother. She didn't know anything about being a mom let alone a decent one. Not to mention being Cullen's wife. She could try, but she would end up failing as before. And that would hurt both of them.

Zoe handed her a glass of water. "Take a sip."

Sarah raised her head and drank.

Christian's gaze never left her face. "Your color's returning."

"I'm feeling better," she said.

But her heart was breaking. Thank goodness her things were packed. If Cullen asked her to stay, she wouldn't be able to leave him. That would turn into a disaster. The longer she stayed, the more it would hurt when it ended. She couldn't do that to Cullen. She wouldn't do that to him.

Or herself.

She had to end things now. No going back again. No matter how tempted she might be.

Sarah glanced at the envelope containing the divorce papers. She didn't know whether they needed to be signed or what. But once she figured it out, she could leave. Cullen hadn't tried to win her back before. He wouldn't this time.

Her heart cried out at the thought.

No, she wouldn't let emotion overwhelm her.

This was for the best. Sarah wasn't strong enough to survive being left again. She wasn't sure she was strong enough to leave him on her own. She would have to leave before he got home.

Sarah drank the rest of her water. "I'm okay now. Really."

The relief on her three friends' face coated her mouth with guilt. But this was for the…best. She would be out of here before Cullen returned.

Coward, a voice inside her mocked.

Not a coward. Smart. Proactive. This was the best way—the only way—to break the hold Cullen had over her and keep her heart safe.

Cullen supposed there were worse places he could be than a snow cave in the middle of a blizzard on Mount Hood with four of his closest friends. Someday he might laugh about this, but not tonight.

At least they were safe. And so were the missing climbers. Three lives had been saved today. No sense risking theirs. As soon as the weather cleared, they would head down. Until then, they would make the best of it.

He sipped from his water bottle. The liquid—melted snow—warmed his insides on this chilly night. He'd rather be cuddling in bed with Sarah.

He missed her. He would miss her more when she left Hood Hamlet.

But Cullen understood. Mount Baker was blowing off steam. He didn't blame her for wanting to be back at the institute.

"Whose bright idea was it to sleep out here?" Hughes asked.

"Paulson's," Porter, Moreno and Cullen said at the same time.

"Just a suggestion." Paulson hunkered down inside his sleeping bag. "I didn't think anyone would take me seriously."

"You know Doc," Porter teased. "He's always serious."

Cullen stuck his water bottle inside his sleeping bag to keep it from freezing. "Someone needs to be serious around you clowns."

Hughes grinned. "I'm sure Doc's all fun and games when he's with Sarah."

"She does keep me smiling." Cullen would give anything to be with her now, to feel her warm body and soft curves snuggled up against him. The thought raised his temperature a degree, maybe two. That might work to his advantage here.

"Being opposites is good," Moreno said. "Rita can't stand anything I like to do except hike. And only when it's sunny and warm. But we're about to celebrate our eighth anniversary."

"Rough life having one gourmet meal after another cooked for you," Hughes said. "Unlike me with a gorgeous wife who can't boil water without the fire department showing up."

"It's amazing Moreno isn't pushing three hundred pounds," Paulson teased.

Moreno smirked. "I burn off the calories other ways."

"Yeah, chasing little Wyatt," Hughes joked.

"That's right," Porter said. "Kids make those long, lazy mornings spent in bed a thing of the past."

Moreno unwrapped a granola bar. "Unless the kids are with you."

Porter nodded. "I can't wait to see my girls. I'd love one of Carly's cookies right now."

"She'll have a plateful at the base when we get down," Hughes said.

Moreno nodded. "And Zoe will be there with piping-hot cups of coffee."

A faraway look filled Hughes's eyes. He tightened

the cord on his jacket's hood. "Too bad she can't deliver up here."

Paulson made a sour-looking face. "Marriage has turned you all into a bunch of saps. Well, except Doc. He's the same as always."

Cullen wasn't sure that was a compliment. He wiggled his fingers to keep them warm.

"Nah," Hughes said. "He smiles more now."

"I actually heard him laugh," Porter teased.

"Very funny, guys," Cullen said.

Things might be up in the air between him and Sarah, but for all their troubles, he couldn't deny he was a better man for having her in his life. She brought spontaneity to his life and tried to make him see what was important, that there was more to living than making plans. Just because he lost control, whether a little or a lot, didn't mean he was going to fall over the edge like Blaine. He wouldn't with Sarah as his anchor.

Even though he was stuck up here, Sarah was the one who kept his thoughts focused. She was good for him. Not dangerous.

Sarah was the one who had soothed his fears about Paulson. She'd been the reason Cullen had opened up when that was the last thing he wanted to do.

Being open was his biggest fear, not being reckless. The people he was closest with, people like

Sarah and Blaine, could hurt Cullen the most and send his emotions out of control. But this second time around with Sarah, being more open with her had made him stronger, not weaker. The same with Blaine's memory.

But Cullen hadn't realized that. Not until now. Would his acknowledging it be enough to keep Sarah from leaving? He didn't know, nor did he care. But he knew one thing. Love was worth the risk.

With a trembling hand, Sarah removed the papers from the white envelope. She scanned each page of the dissolution of marriage petition. Neither of them had any assets the other wanted to claim, so it was pretty cut-and-dried. If she agreed with the petition, she didn't have to respond. The paperwork would go before a judge and their marriage would be over.

With a blue pen in her left hand, she set the tip against a piece of paper. Tears stung the corners of her eyes. Her heart didn't want her to write this note. But she'd learned long ago she couldn't trust her heart.

Sarah refocused, ignoring the pain in her chest. Her heart thudded like a bass drum. The steady beat made her think of a post-battle scene when those who had survived the melee gathered the bodies of dead soldiers. She pushed the graphic image from her mind.

This wasn't war. More like a surrender, a quiet one without any fanfare.

With a shaky hand she wrote what needed to be said and scribbled her signature at the end of the note.

There. She dropped the pen. It was done. Over.

She inhaled, thinking she would feel better. Instead she felt worse.

For the best, Sarah reminded herself. She'd better get busy. The shuttle would be here soon to take her to the airport.

She placed the divorce papers back in the white envelope and set them on the breakfast bar. She placed the note on top.

Last night she'd pulled her wedding ring out of the zippered pocket in her toiletry kit and stuck the gold band on her finger. She'd wanted to wear it one last time. For old times' sake...

Sarah slowly removed the wedding band. The ring slipped off her finger as easily as it had gone on. She placed the gold band with the note and the white envelope. And her heart wept.

CHAPTER FOURTEEN

HOME.

Anticipation pulsed through Cullen's veins. He dumped his backpack in the garage. He would unpack his gear later. All he wanted was to see Sarah.

He entered the house. "Sarah."

She didn't answer.

He searched for her, trying to ignore a sense of foreboding.

She wasn't there.

Shoulders hunched, Cullen walked back to the living room. He understood Sarah's need to return to Bellingham, to her job at the institute. Reporters had been abuzz with news of more steam blasts and earthquakes from Baker. Granted he'd been stuck in a snow cave overnight, but to take off without so much as a goodbye…

A white envelope on the breakfast bar caught his attention.

A two-ton weight pressed down on him. He trudged to the kitchen, feeling as if he were wading through quicksand. He saw a note and a gold wedding band sitting on top of the envelope. With unsteady hands he unfolded the piece of paper and read.

Dear Cullen,

I appreciate all you've done for me these past weeks. Hood Hamlet has been the perfect place to recover. Thank you for opening your home to me and introducing me to your friends.

I know you wanted to drive me home to Bellingham, but after being stuck overnight in a snow cave the last thing you need is to be stuck in a car making the long drive there and back.

The dissolution of marriage petition was served yesterday. I do still want a divorce. I agree with everything in the paperwork and will not be filing a response. Very soon there will be nothing stopping you from getting your life back on track.

I wish you the best. Heaven knows you deserve better than someone like me. I'm sure you'll find her and she'll be exactly what you want in a wife!

Sarah

No! Cullen crinkled the page into a tight ball. He wanted to scream, shout, hit something. He threw the note. It bounced off the wall and fell to the floor. Familiar anger and resentment exploded. Hands shaking, Cullen picked up her wedding ring. He ran his fingers around the smooth gold band. Sarah hadn't seemed like the sentimental type, yet she'd kept hers. As he'd kept his. He set the ring on the bar.

The silence and emptiness of the cabin matched the way he felt inside.

Was this how Sarah had felt when she'd arrived home from doing research on Mount Baker and discovered he'd moved out while she was away? Cullen didn't want to know the answer. She didn't deserve any sympathy.

Damn her. Couldn't Sarah see they had something special? Why would she walk away like this?

He stiffened.

Walk away like he had when she'd brought up a divorce.

Cullen retrieved the wadded-up note, smoothed the wrinkles from the page, then reread it. Again and again. Her words sank in. Something clicked.

Sarah wasn't leaving him for something better. She wanted him to find something—someone—better than her. This wasn't about him or them, but her. For some reason she didn't think she was good enough.

Just like the last time. But he'd been too hurt, too full of pride to realize it.

Snippets of conversations rushed to the surface.

I've never felt so inadequate in my life.

I wasn't anything special. I would have held him back. I don't blame him for not wanting to marry me.

They didn't care about me. They never wanted me around. After the divorce, they shuttled me back and forth.

All the pieces had been there, but Cullen hadn't put them together. Until now.

He needed to go after her and show her how special she was, how much he needed her. Something her mom and dad had never done, or her idiotic fiancé or...

Him.

His chest tightened, squeezing the air out of his lungs. He'd let Sarah down a year ago. No, he'd let her down from the time they'd returned to Seattle from Las Vegas and he'd tried to remain in control after she had rocked his neat and tidy little world. He'd kept parts of his life separate from her. He'd been afraid of losing control, of following in Blaine's footsteps and losing himself to something that would be bad for him, so Cullen had held on tight to what he could and kept her out. What had the family counselor called it? *Compartmentalizing.* He'd taken it a step further. He'd built walls, remained silent and run away.

When Sarah had mentioned divorce, he'd jumped at the chance to make a clean break, then retreated like a turtle into its shell to lick his wounds. What he'd failed to see was how good Sarah was for him. Damn good.

He wasn't going to make the same mistake again. He would go to Bellingham and convince her they belonged together. Do whatever it took. Fight for her if he had to.

At this point he had nothing to lose except...everything.

Sitting at her desk at MBVI, Sarah studied the seismographic signals. Around her, the atmosphere crackled with energy, phones rang at an almost frenetic rate and people carried equipment out of the building in order to set up additional monitoring stations a safe distance away from the volcano.

Seismic activity from inside Mount Baker's crater had quadrupled in frequency since yesterday's steam blast. Whatever was going on could fizzle out, but until that happened she had work to do. Anticipation over the possibilities ahead buzzed through her, but something kept her feet firmly planted on the ground.

Not something. Someone. Cullen.

She leaned back in her chair, not wanting thoughts of him to swamp her.

The new and exciting seismic signals should be her

only concern, but Sarah kept thinking about Hood Hamlet. She missed the town, the people, Cullen. She'd left with so many unknowns.

Had he and the rest of the rescue team made it off the mountain safely? Had he arrived home, read her note? Did he hate her?

Sarah rubbed her tired eyes, then refocused on the data.

Tucker placed a steaming cup of coffee and a chocolate bar on the left side of her desk. "You've been working hard."

The candy reminded her of the chocolate-tasting with Cullen, of his hot kiss. He would never be kissing her again. A knife twisted inside her.

Maybe caffeine would help her concentrate. She took a sip of coffee. "That's why you hired me."

"I hired you because you're qualified and smart." Tucker sat on the right edge of her desk. Her boss was in his late thirties, wore jeans and a T-shirt. He looked more like a rugged cowboy than a nerdy, calculator-toting scientist. "You're also still recovering. Don't overdo it."

"There's lots of data to review."

"And more coming," he admitted. "But you don't have to get through it all right now. Think of it as job security."

She looked up at him. "My funding runs out soon."

"I always have an ace or two up my sleeve. And I have a feeling I'm going to need you around." Tucker had built MBVI from the ground up with lots of sweat and begging and a generous donation from a mysterious anonymous benefactor. He glanced in the direction of Mount Baker. "I'm just relieved you're back. I half expected to receive a call from the Cascades Volcano Observatory asking for a reference so they could hire you."

She flinched. "Why would you think that?"

"Cullen. He was very worried about you at the hospital."

Memories stirred beneath her breastbone. Of him, of her, of them. No, she couldn't go there. "He's a doctor. *Concerned* is his middle name."

"He was more than concerned."

How would Tucker know anything about that? "It doesn't matter. The divorce petition has been filed. I'm not challenging anything. It's over."

"I'm sorry for both of you, but that's one less thing to take you away from here." Tucker stood. "You have one more hour to work. Then go home and sleep."

Her muscles tightened. Steam was still rising from the crater. "I'll sleep when Baker sleeps."

"Now that you're back, I can't afford to lose you."

Her boss's words made Sarah straighten, but they

didn't fill the emptiness inside her. Once she'd found total fulfillment in her work. Now she realized she'd been masking the loneliness, the hurt, the ache left by the failure of her marriage. The loss of Cullen.

"We have to figure out when something else might happen up there," Tucker continued. "You need to be in top form. Rested. Ready for anything. Got it?"

Sarah knew that tone. No worries. She could work remotely from home. "Got it."

"And no working from home, either."

Darn. "Yes, sir."

She returned to the data. Thirty minutes later her forehead throbbed. Eyestrain, tiredness or...a broken heart? Most likely a combination of all three. She massaged her temples.

Maybe Tucker was right about going home. She closed her laptop and slid it into her bag. She said goodbye to her coworkers, then exited the institute.

Outside, she glanced up at Mount Baker. The plume of steam contrasted against the blue sky. A gray, overcast day would have matched her mood and the volcano's much better.

"Sarah."

The sound of Cullen's voice sent chills through her. She turned. He leaned against the building. The sight of him in a pair of faded jeans and short-sleeved T-shirt made her mouth go dry. She had to be way more tired than she realized if she was imagining him here.

Sarah blinked. Still there. She wasn't hallucinating. She pinched herself. Not dreaming, either.

She pursed her lips. "Why are you here?"

He straightened. "You forgot something."

No way. Sarah had been extra careful when she packed, to make sure she had everything that belonged to her. "What did I forget?"

Cullen raised his chin slightly, his jaw tight and his eyes dark. "Me."

Her mouth gaped. The air whooshed from her lungs. She couldn't breathe.

He walked toward her, slowly, as if each step were planned, calculated, with intent and purpose. "You're busy with important work, so I brought me to you."

She tried to speak, but couldn't.

He reached forward and ran his hand along her cheek.

Sarah fought the urge to sink into his touch. She had to be strong. For both their sakes.

His gaze ran the length of her. "You've been working too hard. You have a headache."

How did he know that? Her brain whirled with questions and fatigue and a heavy dose of confusion. "I don't understand why you're here."

Cullen pulled something from behind his back.

It must have been tucked in the waistband of his jeans. A white envelope. The divorce papers. "You left these for me."

Her heart thudded with dread. "We'll be divorced soon."

He held the envelope out in front of him and tore the top portion.

She reached forward to stop him. "What are you doing?"

"What I should have done a year ago and put an end to any talk of a divorce." He ripped the envelope in half. "Worst money I ever spent."

She stared, stunned. "It doesn't matter. The petition has been filed."

"I told my attorney to halt the proceeding."

Her mouth gaped. She closed it. "We'll have to start over."

"That's all I want. For us to start over."

Her heart pounded against her chest. Disbelief and hope warred inside her.

"I don't want a divorce, Sarah. I've never wanted one, but I was too hurt to realize it. I love you. Only you."

"Love is…"

"The only thing that matters." He took her left hand. "I haven't been the best husband. After what happened to Blaine I was afraid to lose control and wind up like him. You overwhelmed me from the moment we met. It was great at first. I felt whole again, but I got scared. Clung to control where I could. Ran away when I couldn't. Didn't open myself up. Compartmentalized everything. My work. My emotions. Our marriage. You. That wasn't right. Or fair. No wonder you wanted to leave. You deserved better from me. I'm finally ready to give it to you. If you want it. Want me."

Cullen's words sent a gush of warmth flowing through Sarah's veins. She fought the urge to soak up the love he was offering. "Oh, I appreciate this. You'll never know how much. But I've seen what's happened with my parents and stepparents. Even if we wanted to make it work, marriage doesn't last."

He squeezed her hand. "I know you've seen marriages fail. You've lived through it way too many times. But the divorce rate isn't one hundred percent. Some marriages do last. Ours can if we're willing to work on it. Fight for it. I know you're a fighter. So am I."

She wanted to believe, but something—fear, maybe—held her back. "Even if we fought for it, I don't know how to be a good wife like Hannah, Carly and Zoe. You need someone who's worthy of you. Perfect for you. That isn't me."

"You might not think you're the perfect wife, but

you're the perfect wife for me." Cullen pressed her hand against his mouth and kissed it. "I was afraid of losing myself in you. The way Blaine lost himself in drugs. What I failed to see is how good you are for me. You're the best thing that's ever happened to me. You fill me up and set me free. You make me stronger. Nothing wrong with that at all."

Her heart sighed. Still more protests rose to her lips. "But—"

"I don't care that you'd rather be covered in mud or ash than wear something frilly. Or that you prefer cooking on a glacier than in a gourmet kitchen. I love that you're willing to run toward an erupting volcano if it means getting the data you need while everyone else is running away. That's the woman I love, the woman I married, the woman I want to grow old with."

Tears stung the corners of her eyes. Feelings of inadequacy shot arrows through her. She sniffled. "But you deserve better."

"You do, too. I'm far from the perfect man or husband. I tend to see things my way. Sometimes I'm too serious."

That made her smile. "Sometimes?"

He grinned. "A lot of times. I don't have a clue how to show how I'm feeling."

Love for this man bubbled in her soul. "You're doing a pretty good job right now."

"It isn't easy," he admitted. "But you're worth it. We both have a lot to learn and work to do. A lot of things can go wrong, but we can make this work. I have no doubt. But we'll never know unless we're willing to take a chance. I am. If you are, I trust you'll stick it out even if things get a little rough. Up for it?"

Hope was starting to win. "I would love to believe our life, our future, could be spent together, not apart."

He kissed her on the lips. "Believe it. Stay my wife."

If ever she had a chance at a forever kind of love, it would be with Cullen. His coming for her proved he knew her, understood her, sometimes better than she knew herself. But fear kept whispering all the things that could go wrong. She was afraid of being disappointed, of being left. But fear wasn't a good enough reason for walking away from something that had the potential to be so wonderful.

"Yes." Sarah was afraid, but willing, oh-so-willing. She kissed him, a kiss full of her hopes and dreams for the two of them. "I love you. I want to make this work more than anything."

His warm breath caressed her skin. He hugged her. "We are going to make this work."

Hope overflowed from her heart. "So what happens now?"

He removed two gold bands from his pocket. He slid hers on her ring finger. "Your turn."

She placed the other on his finger.

"You'll need to show me where we live," he said. "Then I need to get my résumé together and drop a copy off at the hospital."

She stared at him in disbelief. "What?"

"I love living in Hood Hamlet, but I love you more. I want to be where you are, whether it's here by Mount Baker or wherever you end up. Most places need doctors. And we can always go back to Hood Hamlet someday. Or not. Let's play it by ear and see what happens. Plans can be so overrated."

Her heart swelled with love and respect for her husband. "You are amazing, Dr. Gray."

"You're not so bad yourself, Lavagirl."

As Cullen kissed her, the ground trembled. Another earthquake from Mount Baker.

Contentment and joy flowed through Sarah. She didn't need the sparkling castles with gleaming turrets she'd read about as a child. A steam-blasting volcano in the northern Cascades was the perfect backdrop for the beginning of her and Cullen's fairy tale and true love's kiss.

* * * * *